FIRST TIME IN PAPERBACK!

THE MOUNTAIN FUGITIVE

MAX BRAND

**Author of Millions of Books in Print!
"Brand's Westerns are good reading and crammed
with adventure!"
—*Chicago Tribune***

A writer of legendary genius, Max Brand has brought to his
Westerns the raw frontier action and historical authenticity
that have earned him the title of world's most celebrated
Western writer. In *The Mountain Fugitive*, mischief-maker
and town bully Lee Porfilo has a talent for getting himself
into trouble, and it is not long before he's a hunted fugitive—
one step from a hangman's rope.

D0019483

MAX BRAND

THE MOUNTAIN FUGITIVE

LEISURE BOOKS   **NEW YORK CITY**

A LEISURE BOOK®

March 2000

Published in special arrangement with
Golden West Literary Agency.

Published by
Dorchester Publishing Co., Inc.
276 Fifth Avenue
New York, NY 10001

ISBN 0-8439-3574-X

Printed in the United States of America.

THE
MOUNTAIN
FUGITIVE

Chapter One

Leon, Mischief-Maker

I was not born upon Monday, Tuesday, Wednesday, nor upon Thursday, Friday, or Saturday, I presume, because the blessings of those days are mixed; but I came into this world upon a Sunday. I was the only child of a butcher in the town of Mendez, in Arizona. His name was Leon Porfilo, and I was given the same appellation. My mother was Irish, of County Clare. I got my red hair from her and my olive skin from my father. He was not a Mexican. There had not been a cross into a Latin race for generations.

My father was a cunning businessman. He had begun life as a common cowpuncher, and he had saved enough out of his monthly wages to finally buy out a butcher's business in the town of Mendez. You have never heard of Mendez; for my part, I hope that I shall never lay eyes upon it again. It lies on a great flat of burned desert with a cool puff of mountains on the northern horizon, to which

I turned my heart from my infancy.

Whether in rare summer or bitter winter, heat or ice, sun or shade, give me mountains. I would not have any pleasantly rolling hills. I would have mountains that shoot the eye up to heaven one instant and drop it to hell the next. I would take my rides where the wild goats pasture, and roll down my blankets at night, where the sun will find me first in the whole world the next morning.

But as for the desert, I cannot write the word without seeing the sun-scalded town of Mendez once more, and breathing the acrid clouds of alkali dust which were forever whirling through its streets. I cannot hear the word without an ache behind my eyes as I think of stretching a glance toward that million-mile horizon.

It was a dull huddle of houses in which there lived a handful or two of men and women with sallow, withered faces—old at thirty and bowed at fifty. Even the dogs looked unhappy.

I said that I was an only child, which implies that, although I was born on Sunday, I was cursed. An only child is either too good to be true, or a spoiled, pampered devil. I may admit that I was never too good to be true.

My father had just sufficient means to make me wish that he had more. When I asked for a horse, he could give me a pony—and there you are! The more favors he showered on me, the more I hated him, because he did not give me what I craved. He, in the meantime, toiled like a slave.

I rather despised him because he was such a slave.

My mother was true Irish. She loved her religion, and she loved her son with an equally devout enthusiasm. She would have died for the one as readily as for the other. I soon learned her character as well as that of my father. I learned that I could coax anything from her and whine until I got what I wanted from him.

They continued to consider me a blessing sent to them directly from heaven, until I grew big enough to convince the world that I was something else; and I convinced the world long before I convinced my parents.

I was big-boned, square-jawed, and blunt-nosed; the very type to take punishment without feeling it and deal it out heavily in return. School meant to me nothing but a chance to battle, and the school yard was my tournament field. When the teachers complained about me, my lies at home more than offset their bad reports of me. I posed as a statue of injured virtue in my house.

I went on in this way for a good many years, learning nothing but idle habits and loving nothing but my own way. I was fifteen when a turn came in my life.

Young Wilkins, the son of a well-to-do rancher, came into town riding a fine young horse which his father had given him. Half an hour later I had picked a fight with him, thrashed him soundly, and taken the horse as a natural prize of victory. I did not intend to steal the brute, of course. But I intended to give it the ride of its life—and I did. I brought it back to Mendez a couple of hours later, staggering, foaming, and nearly dead. I found it a fine young colt; I left it a wrecked and heartbroken beast which was not worthy of its keep.

Mr. Wilkins looked at the battered face of his son when he came home and said nothing; he felt in common with most Westerners that if their children could not take care of themselves they must accept the penalty. But when he saw the condition of the colt, he had another thought.

He rode to the home of the sheriff and spoke his mind; and the sheriff rode to the home of my father and found him, in the late evening, just returned from his rounds and wearily unharnessing his fagged team.

The upshot of it was that I did not go to jail, but my father had to buy the colt at a handsome price. That outlay of money was a severe tax, and the sight of the useless new horse in the corral every day was a continual goad to both of my parents. They began to inquire among their neighbors, and the moment these good people found that the doors were opened at last, and that Leon Porfilo, the elder, was willing to hear the truth about his offspring, they unburdened themselves of a thousand truths about me. I was described as a lazy ne'er-do-well, a consummate idler, a stupid bully, a foolish student, and a professional mischief-maker in the town.

"The hangman usually gets youngsters that start out like this!" said the most outspoken of all.

My father came home to my mother and told her everything. There was a storm of tears and of protests; and then my mother sent for the priest. He listened to her patiently. He did not offer to advise her; he did not corroborate the reports of the loose-tongued neighbors; but he said, when she asked him what she could do with me:

"Give young Leon to me for six months. I shall guarantee to teach him his lessons, reform his manners in part, and give him a certain measure of industry."

My mother was enraptured.

"But," continued Father McGuire, "I shall expect a return for these services."

My mother told him that he could ask whatever he wanted, and that Leon Porfilo would be glad to pay.

"I do not want a penny," said Father McGuire. "If I cannot make that young man pay for his lessons and his keep and the trouble I am forced to expend on him, my name is not McGuire! Only, I insist that I shall have absolute and unquestioned charge of him from the first

day to the end of six months. During that time you are
not to lay eyes upon him.

"At the end of that time, you may see him, and if you
like his progress and what he will have to tell you about
me and my methods of teaching, you may leave him in
my hands for a longer time. If you do *not* like my way
with him, you may have him back, and I shall wash my
hands of the matter."

This was a great thing to ask of my mother. I am
certain that she could not have consented had it not been
that she could not understand the priest's reasons for
wishing to take me on such unusual terms. Because what
he demanded was a mystery, it overcame any possible
objections on the part of either of my parents. Finally,
they asked me if I were willing to go to the priest's house
and to live with him.

I considered my picture of the priest's life, his comfortable little house, his neat garden filled with well-watered,
well-tended flowers, his sheds, always freshly painted, his
larder always well-filled with good cookery, and above
all the thin, patient, weary face of little Father McGuire
himself. A sense of my own bulk overwhelmed me. Any
change would have been delightful to me.

I consented at once, and the next day my clothes and
books, my whole list of possessions down to my latest
fishing rod, were bundled together, and I was sent away
to the house of Father McGuire.

I was let into the house by the old servant, a half
blind woman who had worked for so many years in that
house that she found her way about more by the sense
of touch than anything else, I am sure. The sight of her
was satisfactory to me. I decided that it would be a simple
matter for me to hoodwink her at every turn. She told me
that Father McGuire half expected me and that, since he

was away making the rounds of his parish—for he was an indefatigable worker for his church—I was to make myself at home and spend the day becoming accustomed to the place and all that was in it.

In the meantime she showed me my room.

I was delighted with it. It was not half so large as my chamber at home. It was in the second story of the little building, and it had a tiny dormer window which looked to the north, but all was as neat as a pin, the floor was freshly painted, the bed was newly made and covered with a crisp white spread, and past the window ran the delicate tendrils of the only successfully raised climbing vine that had ever graced the town of Mendez.

There was a small cupboard where I could put away my gear and my books—the books which I intended to keep as much strangers to me as they had ever been in the past. There was a closet where I hung out my clothes, and then I made a survey of the house and the grounds.

The house itself lay on the edge of the town, near the church. Its grounds were as small, comparatively, as the house in which the good priest lived. In a land where acres could be had almost for the asking, the priest had contented himself with a tiny plot which included room for a flower garden around the house and a vegetable patch behind it, then a wood and cattle shed, and finally a pasture just large enough to maintain the one musty-looking old pony and the cow, which was a comfortable brindle.

My first amusement was to whistle to a passing dog and set it on the cow, and I laughed until my sides ached at the manner in which she went hurtling around the lot, tossing her horns, helpless, with her great udder swinging from side to side.

Then, when I was satisfied with this amusement, I strolled back to the house and, passing the open kitchen window, purloined a delicate blackberry tart which was cooling on the sill.

Chapter Two

The First Lesson

All the rest of that day went as pleasantly as the commencement of it, and in the evening, almost at as late an hour as my father returned from his rounds, the priest came wearily home to the house. He greeted me with a smile and a firm handshake with such strength in it that I wondered at him. For he seemed to have a most athletic hand!

We sat down to supper together, and while we ate he talked with me and asked me little questions about myself and what I intended to do with my life.

"I believe," said the good priest, "that after a boy has reached a certain age, he should be allowed to do as he pleases with his life. In the meantime, I should like to find out what you *now* please to do with yourself."

I told him, glad to talk of myself, that I intended to grow larger and stronger, and that I then intended to look about me and find a place where one did not have to work too much in the hot sun. Indoor work would suit me.

"You wish to become a student, then?" suggested Father McGuire.

I admitted that books were extremely distasteful to me, and that I did not desire to have any intimate knowledge of them, whatsoever.

There was no more talk on these subjects. Father McGuire turned his attention to other things. He declared that he had heard a great deal about my fights with other boys, and he particularly mentioned a few recent instances. I admitted sullenly that I had fought occasionally, and that I hoped that I would soon get over that bad habit.

"By no means," said Father McGuire, who seemed to have recovered from his languor of weariness. "By no means! Those men whom I most admire in this world are the saints who bless it with their gentleness. But they are very few." Here he sighed.

"I have seen only two or three in all my life. But next to the saints, I love the warriors, of which there are always a fair number—I mean the true hearts of oak who will fight until the ship sinks! Perhaps you are to be one of those, Leon!"

It was a thrilling possibility—when I heard him speak of it in this manner. I began to regard myself as a great man, and when that pleasant evening ended, I went to bed and to sleep without the slightest regret that I was not in the house of my parents. I decided that Father McGuire would never thwart a single one of my wishes.

In the morning, a full three hours before my ordinary time of waking—which was eight—I heard a brisk rap at the door, and the cheerful voice of Father McGuire in the hall, telling me that it was time to get up.

"Get up?" said I, sitting up in the bed and blinking at the dull gray of the sky outside my window, "why, it's the middle of night."

He told me that he had some good news for me; and that brought me out of bed in a twinkling. In an instant I had leaped into my clothes, and I was standing before him in the hall.

"You are to learn to milk," said Father McGuire, who had remained there waiting for me all of this time. "I intend to teach you this morning."

I made a wry face, not too covertly, and went along with him to find the cow. For ten or fifteen minutes, I pretended to attempt to do as he told me. As a matter of fact, I had done a little milking before, and could perform fairly well at it. For the priest, however, I pretended that it was a hopeless task for me; I wished to discourage, in the beginning of our acquaintance—which was bound to last for at least six months—this foolish habit of rousing me before daybreak to do chores about the house.

Suddenly the hand of Father McGuire was laid upon my shoulder. "Will you tell me the truth?" he asked.

"Yes," said I.

"Are you doing your best?"

I declared that I was, and made an apparently savage effort to get the milk from the udder of the cow. But there was not a trickle in answer. I told Father McGuire that it was no good; and that I could not master the knack of the thing. He smiled upon me in the gentlest manner.

"There is no hurry," said he. "In these things, one must use the most infinite patience. It is very true that one often needs time, but time, after all, is often a cheap matter in this world of ours. It may require an hour, or two hours— but it is a long time, as I said—before breakfast. Sit there and do your best. I cannot ask any more."

He folded his arms and leaned against the fence, watching me. I began to perspire with impatience and anger. My back was aching from that infernally cramped position, and in another moment, as by magic, all the difficulties disappeared, and the streams of milk began to descend with a rhythmic chiming into the pail—then with increasing force as I set aside all pretense, and hurried to finish the task.

Father McGuire stood by and admired. He had never seen such an apt pupil, he declared.

"Which teaches one," said he, "that a slow beginning often makes a good ending!"

The cow was milked; I carried the pail sullenly to the house and dropped it on the floor, but Father McGuire was not yet done with me. I was shown how I must strain it into three pans; and how I must take down the pans of yesterday from the little creamery and skim them, and throw the cream into the cream jar, and then empty the skimmed milk into another pail.

After that, I was led forth to the pasture again and told to catch the horse. The horse became exceedingly difficult to capture. It seemed impossible for me to manage the brute, and I told Father McGuire as much.

His answer made me begin to hate him.

"More gently, then," said he. "But always with patience, my dear Leon. The time will come when she will come straight up to your hand. She is a gentle creature, although a very stupid one. See what time accomplished in the matter of learning how to milk! It may do even more in this affair of the catching of the horse."

I saw that I was fairly trapped, and that he intended to let me learn in my own way. So I caught the stupid beast at once and led her into the barn. I was told to curry and brush her, and Father McGuire showed me how to proceed. I snatched the brush and comb when he offered them to me, and began to work in a blind passion.

"Wait! Wait! Wait!" said the gentle voice of the priest. "More haste and less speed! You must not curry *against* the grain—but so——"

I flung brush and comb upon the floor with a loud clatter. "I'm not a slave!" cried I. "I won't do any more."

He raised his pale hand. "Not that word, my dear Leon," said he. "'Won't' is the one word of all others which I detest in a boy. The point is that I have told you to brush and curry the horse. For stupidity I trust that I have an infinite patience; but for willful obstinacy I desire a sword of fire. Do not provoke me, Leon. Do not let anger take the upper hand with me. Let anger be far from me, always, in my treatment of you!"

He actually raised his eyes as he was saying this, as though it were a manner of prayer. At this, my rage broke through.

"You little runt!" I yelled at him. "I'm gonna leave, and I'm gonna leave right now!"

I started for the door.

"Will you come back, Leon?" said the gentle voice.

"I'll see you go to the devil first," said I.

A light step followed me; a hand of iron gripped my arm and flung me around.

"Go back to your work," said Father McGuire through his teeth. He pointed toward the long-suffering horse.

I was enraged by that grip upon my arm from which my muscles still ached. Though I have never been the type of bully that picks upon younger boys, I now forgot myself. I struck heavily at the head of Father McGuire.

My father or my mother would have fainted with horror to see such a blow leveled at the man of God, but there was no fainting in Father McGuire. His small arms darted out, my wrist landed against a sharp elbow so that I howled with the stabbing pain of it, and the next moment a bony little fist darted up and nestled against the very point of my jaw.

There was an astonishing weight behind that hand. It lifted me from my feet, toppled me backward, and landed me against the wall of the barn with a crash.

There I lay in a stupor, gazing at this man who had worked a miracle.

I should have said that at fifteen, like many others who grow large, I had my full height of an inch above six feet, and I had a hundred and sixty pounds of weight to dress my inches. I had not done hard labor, at that time, and my strength had not been seasoned and hardened upon my shoulders, but still I was a stout youngster.

But here was I, full of consciousness of my hundred and sixty pounds of victorious brawn, laid flat on my back by a blow delivered by the fist of a little withered priest who had not three quarters of my bulk.

I say that I lay flat on my back and glared at him with a chill of dread working in my blood. He, in the meantime, was standing before me with a great emotion in his face. He was flushed, his teeth were set, his feet were braced well apart beneath his robe, and there was a strange glitter in his eyes.

"Let me not lose myself, Lord," said Father McGuire. "Let me not sin in passion. Let me be tender, and turn my other cheek to the smiter! Fill me with humility, Our Father——"

Here I leaped to my feet with a roar and rushed at him, and Father McGuire, with a little indrawn breath of pleasure, as of one drinking deep of happiness, met me with what any instructor in boxing would have termed a beautiful straight left.

Chapter Three

One Fortnight

The straight left, as all men know, is to boxing what rhythm is to poetry. It is the foundation upon which all the other beauties are based and erected; it is the chief substance which the true artist will use. Now, I had fought my way up through the ranks of valorous boys, each the making of a future tough-handed cow-puncher and bull-dogger. But in all that time I had never encountered, and I certainly had never mastered, the fine art of the straight left which starts with a forward drive of the body, and lands with a stiffened arm, the hand twisting over and landing with the fingers down, the line of wrist, shoulder, hip, and right heel being as nearly as possible in one line.

I, leaping in with eagerly flailing arms, found that straight left darting through my guard. It landed on my chin, and I felt as though I had raced in the darkness against a brick wall. My feet skidded from beneath me, and I sat down with a sickening jar.

Through rather glassy eyes I stared up to Father McGuire. He was in a strange condition. He was dancing back and forth with a little jerky, uneasy step that is never learned except on the floor of a gymnasium, with a skillful teacher guiding. His hands were raised to the correct position for renewing the encounter; his face was more flushed than ever, and a queer smile played around the corners of his mouth, while his eyes were literally filled with fire.

My second fall did not convince me any more than my first. It merely bewildered and infuriated me. It was a juggling trick that had put me down by chance, and in my strong young body I felt the existence of an infinite treasure of might. I bounded to my feet again and prepared to smash the priest to bits, no matter if I should have to hang for it.

So I closed with him, took a stinging blow that cut my cheek and knocked my head far back, and got my arms well around him. Now let sheer might tell its own story! Alas, it was like embracing a greased pig—to use an ancient and unsavory simile. The good priest slid or twisted from my embrace, and with a sudden grip, a sudden twist, he flung me over his hip and landed me on my head.

Through a partial daze I heard him shouting:

"Are you well named, boy? Are you a young lion? Are you a lion in heart? Then I am Daniel! I fear you not! But avoid me, if you wish to keep——"

I whirled to my feet, a complete bulldog, now, savage for blood. I ran in through a rain of blows which stunned and cut and bruised me, but once more I came to grips with him. Once more I felt that sudden twisting of his body, which seemed to turn to iron under my touch; and suddenly I was down again. This time, in falling, the back of my head collided with the floor with a loud crash, and I was dropped into a deep well of blackness.

I recovered to find my face and breast and throat dripping with water, while out of the dim distance I heard a voice crooning:

"So, lad, and are you better now?"

The sense of where I was, what had happened, and how I had been beaten, rushed suddenly over me. I started up to my feet.

"I'll break your head, your trickster!" I yelled through swollen lips. "I'll——"

"Ah, Leon,!" said the priest to me. "If you strike me now, Leon, you strike a lamb. Here am I!"

He opened his arms and presented himself patiently for the blow.

But I, struck dumb by this sudden change, and overwhelmed more than ever with the bitterest shame, broke into tears and hid my face in my hands. I found the arm of Father McGuire hooked beneath mine. He led me gently toward the house; I was too blinded by my tight-swollen eyes and my tears to see the way! I was too oppressed in spirit to resist him. The old woman met us at the back door.

She gasped at the sight of me, and I heard the priest say in his gentle voice:

"Our poor Leon, Mimsy. It is a shocking thing! We must take the very best care of him! Get a piece of raw beefsteak, Mimsy, and bring it at once to his room!"

So he took me up and made me lie down on the bed, whose covers he smoothed for me with a quick hand. Then he stretched a blanket over me and sat down by the bed.

"Ah, Leon," he said, patting my hand in his, "do not be ashamed. It is a science, lad, and nothing else. It is the science that makes the little man the equal of the big man—science of hands, science of brains. Work and patience and application will move mountains—even the mountains of a great heart and a warlike spirit, such as yours, my dear boy. Let us be friends!

"Let us be kind to one another! I did not know what was in you. But now I have seen it. There is a great lump of steel. It is not yet modeled; it is not a tool with a cutting edge or a striking face. It has neither been edged nor tempered; it has not been whetted; it has not been fitted to the hand. Give me your time and your trust and we shall do great things together. Give me your faith, Leon, and I shall make you a lion indeed!"

I heard him vaguely. My heart was too great and too thoroughly broken with shame, to heed all the meaning of his words at that moment; for I hated him then all the more, because he had beaten me down and then remained to soothe me.

Presently the good Mimsy hobbled up to the door, and the priest took from her what she brought. I was soon bandaged and padded; and the priest was sucking in his breath and making a clucking noise of commiseration and regret, as he saw how my bruises swelled and my cuts bled.

After he had finished, he begged me to rest easily and try to forgive him. Then he left me.

What I first thought of was waiting until the next midnight and then setting fire to the house in a dozen places to insure the destruction of the priest and Mimsy both—those witnesses to my humiliation. Then I determined to flee at once to my home. But I remembered how terribly my face was battered, and knew that I could not offer any suitable explanation. If it were known that the small hands of the little priest had brought me down and pommeled me, I felt that my reputation was lost forever. Last of all, I desired to die, and quit this vale of sorrows at once and forever.

The result of it all was that I saw myself condemned to remain at the priest's house—and remain very closely there—until my marks of battle had disappeared. And that might take two weeks! I decided to endure patiently and await my chance.

I saw little of Father McGuire on that day, but the next morning he roused me a little before five, as he had done before, and took me out to the chores. I submitted silently and went through with them one by one, he, all the while, giving directions in the most cheerful manner, as though there had never been anything but the best of good feeling between us.

After breakfast, for which I had acquired a good appetite, I was ushered into the library in my turn, and my books were placed before me.

It was not difficult work, at first; it required nothing but the expenditure of time and pains. I began again at the beginning, with first-grade work, which I scorned. I had to learn to write again. I had to learn to spell, again. I had to skim through simple arithmetic, in which my errors were caught up with a skillful eye. From half past eight until twelve o'clock I kept at this work.

Then we had lunch together, after which I washed and wiped the dishes, and was allowed a nap until two o'clock. After two o'clock, I had two hours and a half additional study. After that, Father McGuire sometimes came home and instructed me in certain branches of knowledge which I preferred very much to books. In other words, he unburdened himself of all the secrets which he had learned in his own youth from excellent boxing instructors.

He taught me the secrets of wrestling. For the first time I heard such terms as half nelson, and hip lock. He fitted part of one of the sheds with athletic appliances and a padded floor where he and I struggled several days a week with the gloves or on the mat. There I battered the punching bag to gain speed; there I tussled with the sand bag to gain strength.

So the fortnight ended and my wounds from the first battle were healed.

I was equipped, by this time, with the beginning of a little furrow between my eyes—a mark of increased seriousness and an interest in life. I had stripped off five or six pounds of fat by my arduous labors. I had within me the pulse and the rioting spirit of a man in perfect physical condition.

I was now prepared to leave the priest forever. That day, accordingly, instead of going into the library to study, after breakfast, I went up to my room and gathered my belongings together. But when I had them bundled up, I paused and sat down to think things over.

The prospect of leaving Father McGuire was no longer so attractive. I spent an hour turning the thought back and forth through my mind, and I ended by going slowly down to the library. There I could not study. Noon came before I was aware, and the slender form of the priest appeared in the doorway. He came, as usual, to look at my morning's work, and when he saw that I had not touched pen to paper, I waited with a frown for an outburst.

Instead, he laid a friendly hand upon my shoulder. When I looked up hastily to him, I found that he was smiling upon me.

"I think that the time of storm and struggle is over, Leon," said he. "I think that you are prepared to like me almost half as well as I like you. Are you not?"

I have heard a great deal said of the sensitiveness of girls; but my observation leads me to conclude that boys are far more highly strung. At any rate, on this occasion, I had to look down suddenly to the paper before me, which I found obscured by a thick mist. But Father McGuire walked softly from the room without another word to me.

Chapter Four

A Chance Meeting

From that moment I began to worship the little man. I began to work with a feverish interest at the things which he put before me. At noon and at night he corrected my studies and read aloud to me, and encouraged me through the difficult knots which I had found in various problems. But what I have often wondered at, was that he never forced religion upon me.

He sometimes selected pleasant tales out of the Bible and read these to me and clothed the figures in real flesh for my boy's mind. Sometimes he invited me to the church to listen to the organ music. But further than this he did not go, though I have no doubt that he intended to do much for me in this direction, before the end came to my happy life with him.

Time, as the saying has it, took wings. I had been three months with him in a trice. A certain stock of his lessons I had picked up so successfully that one day, as we boxed, he was forced to cry out to me: "Not so hard, Leon. Well, confound you, take that!"

The rapierlike left darted toward me. I blocked it perfectly and returned a sharp counter to his face with the thick gloves. Thick gloves, but Father McGuire was shaken to the toes. He dragged off the gloves and sat down to rub his cheek.

"Goliath," said he, grinning at me with twinkling eyes, "you must remember that I am a very elderly David!"

So I had my triumph. So I had my revenge for that heavy beating which he had given me. The revenge was so complete that my heart overflowed with it; I found myself apologizing gravely, and without smugness!

"Nonsense!" said Father McGuire. "I am not hurt. But neither do you know your strength. Oh, lad, lad, when you grow into your strength——"

He took one of my boyish arms and ran his own hard finger tips down the courses of the muscles.

My six months ended, and I went home for the first time to my father and my mother; and, for the first time, I saw them as they were. I think it was the saddest and the happiest moment of my life. For I realized as I sat before them that there was a great gap between them and me, and I realized, also, that they were two mines of kindness and whole-heartedness.

They were delighted with the transformation which Father McGuire had worked in me. They were delighted to see some of the loutishness gone. When we sat at the table together, they still were exclaiming and looking at me with fond eyes.

But I was glad to go back to the priest's house on the next day.

"So soon, my dear Leon?" said he.

"Is it too soon?" said I.

"No," said he, "for you may see them whenever you choose from this time on."

In this fashion I became a regular member of the household of Father McGuire. From my fifteenth to my eighteenth year, that long time of study and work continued. Then the blow fell.

It was not the deaths of my father and my mother. Those occurred in my sixteenth year. My father's team—which was a new pair of half-broken mustangs—ran away and overturned the wagon. He was crushed beneath it and was found dead the next day. And only two weeks later my mother died of a weak heart.

These were two heavy blows to me, but still they did not bring on the crisis which had an element of tragedy in it.

Father McGuire, as my guardian, sold the butcher's business, which my father had built up, for a good round price, and then sold the house and the horses and the few cattle. The resulting sum was a little over eight thousand dollars, and I felt myself rich, indeed.

But, a month from the day of my father's death, these transactions being completed, I begged Father McGuire to accept the whole mass of wealth.

"Use this money however you wish," said I to him. "I want to pay it to you to hire you as my teacher. Will you do that? Will you take it and let me come back to live with you as I have lived before?"

He looked at me with such a smile of happiness as I think few men have ever seen. But he would not take a penny of the money. By him it was banked in my name where the savings could accumulate. In the meantime, I was welcomed back to him.

"Because," said he, "I should have to keep a hired man, if it were not for you, Leon!"

So I resumed my life with Father McGuire and Mimsy, who seemed to grow no older—she had reached that point in life where a year or two more or less made no difference. She was unchanging.

But in the meantime, the crisis had been gathering slowly about me.

It began after I had been with Father McGuire something over eight months. I was hurrying down the crooked, ugly little street of the town when I came on some youngsters of my own age playing an improvised form of football, in which the chief fun was seeing how hard the other fellow could be tackled and how many men could jump on him at the same instant as he went down.

Sitting on a fine horse at the side of the street was a handsome, strong-shouldered boy a year or so older than myself. I had grown serious, too serious, perhaps, in my time with Father McGuire. So I took no share in the fun. I stood by, as the stranger did, and laughed at the tumbles and falls.

Suddenly the shadow of horse and rider loomed across me. I looked up into his fine, sneering face.

"Are you afraid of the rest of 'em?" he asked me.

I merely smiled. I was too well known in Mendez to fear the imputation which lay behind this speech.

"What about yourself?" I said to him.

"Not in these clothes," said he. "They're a lot too good to be spoiled roughing it like that."

He indicated with a sweep of the hand all his finery— which was enough to have filled the eye of a Mexican cow-puncher and delighted the heart of his ladylove.

"Things that are too good to play in are a lot too good to wear at all!" said I, for in spite of all the teachings of Father McGuire, I was full of impatience and hotness under the skin.

The tall fellow on the horse pressed himself a little closer to me, so that I had to give ground for his horse. I have said that he was handsome—yes, with a blond sort of beauty such as one finds very rarely, and eyes of as richly deep a blue as might have been wished for in a girl. So, sitting magnificently above me, he smiled on me. He was seventeen. I was sixteen. I was big for my age; he was still larger. As he came closer and felt the superiority of his size and his spirit, he smiled at me again, in his sneering way.

"I'll tell you this, young fellow," said this splendid rider, "no matter what sort of clothes I have on, I've never had any that were too good for a fight!"

"Is that so?" said I, glaring at him. "Come down, then, and give me a square crack at you, and I'll show you how to muss up good clothes so's they're not fit to wear again."

He came like a flash of light from the sky. His feet had hardly struck the ground before he was at me, and I heard a wild yell of excitement from the boys playing in the street:

"Hey! Everybody come look! It's Lee Porfilo and Harry Chase! This'll be the best ever!"

He did not strike me fairly as he came leaping in; I had not been practicing every day with Father McGuire and at the bag and the sand sack for nothing. If one can block the back-flick of a darting punching bag, one has at least a fair chance to block the swing of a fist. I put aside a quick thrusting of punches, and then he closed with me.

The weight of his attack sent a thrill of fear through me. I have never felt the contact of any one which was so overwhelming as that of Harry Chase; except for his brother after him. But they had one thing in common that was above mere considerations of paltry poundage and physical might. They had an immense confidence and a swelling of the spirit that made them fairly override other men as a horse might trample down a boy. So the lunge and pressure of Harry Chase baffled and awed me.

I grew weak, and I staggered back before the shock of his charging weight, so that the chorus of my friends in the street, most of whom had felt the weight of my fists at one time or another, wailed: "Leon is beat! Lee is beat at last!"

Harry Chase, with a swinging cuff of his left fist, clipped me on the chin and sent me reeling still farther away, to verify that first cry. You will not think that the boys of Mendez were very fond of me—seeing that I had always been the town bully and the town ruffian until I went to live with the priest; but I was their champion, and the home champion, no matter what his character may be, is usually favored to win. They watched with held breath or with groans, while Harry Chase drove me before him.

I think that I should have gone down at once before this berserk rush, had it not been for the training of Father McGuire. Such training at last becomes an instinct and takes even the place of courage. By very force of habit I warded off most of the blows which leveled at me. Then, as I saw that I was keeping my own against this lionlike rush, and as I listened to the groans of shame which my companions of the town raised, I shook off my coldness of heart, and prodded at Harry Chase with that straight left which was almost a religious article in the athletic creed of good Father McGuire.

It landed. There is nothing so difficult to avoid as a jabbing, long-range left hand. It is always held out so far that it is very near the mark, in the first place. It is sent home without a preliminary drawing back of the hand to give warning.

I spoiled the next rush of Harry Chase by spatting my stiff left against his mouth, and then, as he gave back and rushed again, he caught the identical punch in the same place twice more. The third time brought a little trickle of blood and a yell of triumph from the little crowd of spectators. In fact, that crowd had been increased by others and older people crowding to doors and windows. Others, still, came running. When boys are sixteen and seventeen, the fun of their fighting is enough to draw even a crowd of mature men.

The sting of his lips, and the surprise of my counterattack, took the last of Harry's sense of caution. He was maddened, just as much as I was warmed by self-confidence. I saw his nostrils flare and his eyes widen to the glare of a bull. He came in with his hands down, and I braced myself and took my time. I did not even have to time and check him with my left. I let him come wildly in and then clipped him with a beautiful right. It went as straight as the left, but it had just three times as much power, because it traveled just three times as far and as fast.

This punch nailed him high on the cheek. Had it been an inch lower and nailed him on the jaw bone, the fight would have ended right there, and I know that if it had ended there, the troubles of the rest of my life would probably have been avoided, also. But after all, I begin to think that there was fate behind it—not my own will.

At any rate, that blow was enough to knock him flat on his back with a force that drove the dust spurting out like water under the impact of his big body. But if he were dazed, he was not badly hurt. He scrambled to his feet at once, while I stood back and dropped my hands on my hips. I knew, now, that the game was in my hands.

This fellow was big and very powerful, with just as much or more natural strength than I had; but he lacked the training and he lacked the seasoning of hard work which I had been doing in Father McGuire's gymnasium.

So I stood back as he came rather uncertainly to his feet, and I sang out to the boys: "If any of you fellows are friends of this gent, call him off, before I do him a harm!"

There was no interference. He who attempted to take the fight off my hands would simply have been transferring it to his own responsibility. My speech affected Harry Chase as a sort of stinging challenge, or a mockery. He came at me with the snarl of a wild cat.

"I'll about kill you for that!" said Harry uncharitably.

I hit him easily away from me with the left again.

"I don't want to do this," said I to the little crowd. "You see that he's got me cornered, and that he won't quit."

But they were delighted. They only yelled: "Give him the devil, Leon!"

He was only a stranger, you see, and much too big a stranger for any of the other boys to handle. Now I am ashamed to confess that I did not mean what I had said. I had not the slightest desire to stop fighting. It was a full eight months since these fellows had seen me at work with my hands, and during those eight months I had been accumulating scientific fighting knowledge hand over hand.

It was the secret desire which swelled in my heart to use this big chap as a chopping block and carve out of him a perfect demonstration of my ability. I wanted to dazzle them, and I set about doing it. At any time I could have put a merciful end to the sufferings of gallant Harry Chase by snapping across a long right-hander to the jaw. But I wouldn't do it. I started out to use him for my object lesson.

He made a perfect subject. He was thrashing away with his hands in a manner that would have taken the heart out of every other boy in town. In fact, my audience stood aghast at the coolness with which I circled this madman as he raged, and, dipping in and out, picked at him with blows that shook him like hammer strokes. They thought that it was very gallant upon my part; they thought that I was the bravest boy in Arizona, by all odds.

Of course I was simply taking advantage of the things which Father McGuire had taught me. I knew that those tremendous round-arm swings, after the style of the very blows which I myself had formerly used, were quite of no avail against a straight hitter who kept his wits about his head and his feet active beneath him.

I danced about Harry Chase, slithering in and out through his thrashing arms, putting by his savage blows with cool parries, stepping back to let thundering sweeps whir past my face the split part of an inch away, and ducking under honestly intentioned knockout blows so that they skimmed my very hair and ruffled it but did no further harm.

"Look at Leon!" my friends yelled. "He ain't got a mark on him!"

In contrast—there was poor Harry Chase! I did not drive at the body, for fear of slowing him down. Punishment about the face stings more and saps the strength less. I had cut and dazed him, but he was as strong as ever. I had kept my promise of spoiling his clothes.

Still he swabbed off his face with a quick hand, squinted at me out of his half-shut left eye—the right was a tight-closed mass of purple—and charged again, only to be knocked, spinning, away.

Then I heard the voice of the sheriff, cutting through the noisy exultation of the boys in the street. I heard the sheriff calling: "Stop that massacre!"

In another moment he would be on us and end the fight while Harry was still on his feet, and that I could not allow. He was rushing again, his mouth open, his face hideous but determined, and I stepped in and caught him with a full shot with the right hand, which lodged just beside the point of the chin, with all my weight, and all my lunging power, and all the whip of my strong arm behind it.

Harry was tossed to the side like a feather before a puff of wind, and he lunged face down into the dust, where he lay without a quiver.

The next instant the sheriff reached him with a bound. He scooped one arm under him as he raised the boy, he pointed his other hand grimly at me: "You, Porfilo—you stay here. I'm gonna have a talk with you!"

I remained. The glory of victory was still a sweet taste in my mouth.

The face of poor Harry Chase had looked bad enough before his last fall. But now, as the sheriff lifted the inert mass, the dust-clotted crimson on Harry's skin, his closed eyes, his thick, bleeding lips, made him look like a frightful caricature of humanity rather than the very handsome fellow he really was.

The sheriff, tough fellow though he was, was shocked.

"Who the devil is it?" he asked.

"Harry Chase," said some one.

"Chase's kid!" cried the sheriff with an oath, and he turned a baleful eye upon me.

I should explain that Mr. Chase had moved into the community only a scant week before, and had spent part of his huge fortune to buy a great tract of range land. There is a difference between beating to a pulp the town boys, and attacking the son of a millionaire, a pillar of the church and of law and order in general. The sheriff's eye boded ill for me, but he said not a word until he had swabbed off the face of the boy and forced a sip of brandy between his lips.

Harry was completely knocked out. It was several minutes before he could stand on his feet, and another minute or two before his head was sufficently cleared to thrust him on the back of his dancing horse, which seemed to understand the indignity and the shame through which his master had just passed.

"Now tell me the rights of this, Harry Chase," said the sheriff. "How did it begin?"

"The talking I'll do about this," said Harry through his thickly mumbling lips, "will be with my fists—another day."

He gave me a look as dark as he could make it through his narrowed slits of eyes. Then he climbed into the saddle and was off as fast as he could ride.

The sheriff turned to the rest of us. "You're not through yet, Porfilo," said he. "Boys, what sort of a club has he been usin' on the face of poor young Chase? Tell me the truth!"

"Only his fists!" they chirped.

The sheriff gave me a gloomy look and, coming to me, he took my hands and examined my knuckles. They were badly skinned from the battering-ram service which had been exacted from them.

"Was this a fair fight?" asked the sheriff, staring at me, but obviously asking of the others.

"Why, Chase began it!" piped a chorus. "Leon, he begged Chase to keep off of him, and Chase wouldn't!"

The sheriff paused. Then he said to me: "All right, kid. But this here sort of fightin' ain't boy stuff no more. You've growed too big. Watch yourself, Porfilo, or you'll be in trouble—bad—one of these days!"

I suppose that I might call it my entrance into manhood, that speech of the sheriff's. Also, it was a prophecy.

Chapter Five

Father M'Guire Questions

That battle crowned me with a very new sort of glory. The other youngsters of Mendez had seen me rush into fights and absorb perhaps more punishment than I gave out until I battered the other fellow down by simply bulldogging my way through to the end. But this was very different. Style once seen, cannot be mistaken, and the clean-cut hitting and blocking and footwork which they had watched in me was a thrilling thing to my compatriots of Mendez. That day was a continual triumph to me, until I came back to the house of Father McGuire.

There was something in his mind; I could tell that by the way he looked at me, but it seemed at first to be entirely jovial.

"I hear," said the good priest, "that you have had a fight with big Harry Chase."

"Where did you hear that?" said I, as any vain boy would have asked.

"The whole town is talking of very little else," said Father McGuire. "You gave him a fine thumping, Leon?"

He smiled at me. It seemed to me that I could feel his pride in me, and I expanded and swelled under the warmth of it.

"He had enough before the finish," said I, and I was eager to tell him more. I wanted to dig into the details of that battle. There was no one else on the whole cattle range, I felt, who could understand the fine points of the work which I had done; there was no one else with whom it was really worth while to talk.

Father McGuire took out his pipe and stuffed it carefully.

"Well," he said at last, "you had a big job on your hands, I see!"

"Why?" said I.

"Why? Because he was older. Isn't he nineteen or twenty years old?"

"He's seventeen—or maybe eighteen," said I.

"But then he's much larger. I suppose he's fifteen or twenty pounds heavier than you are?"

"Not ten," said I.

Father McGuire shook his head. "Nevertheless it was a risky business," said he. "Here was a fellow older, heavier, and stronger than you are——"

"Who said that he is stronger than I?" I exclaimed.

"Ah, but he must be, Lee. He has such a reputation!"

"I dunno what gave him the reputation," said I aggressively, for I hated the imputation that any boy of my own age or thereabout might be greater in sheer might of hand than I.

"Well," said Father McGuire, "we know that he's the younger brother of the famous Andrew Chase——"

I was hugely impressed by this. As a matter of fact, I

had not heard anything about the Chase family in particular since they had come into our section of the range. But of a certain Andrew Chase I had heard vague reports from time to time.

"But Andrew Chase is a middle-aged man, isn't he?" said I.

Father McGuire smiled. "Will you call twenty-one, middle-age?" said he.

"Ah? Is he only that age? How have we happened to hear so much of him? Has he been a killer? Is he still?"

I was swelling with enthusiasm. Father McGuire looked a little sadly, a little sternly, upon me.

"I hope that you never have to know Andrew Chase any better than you know him now," said he. "As a matter of fact, he has not been a killer. Andrew is a hero, my boy."

"What has he done?" said I.

"I hardly know," smiled Father McGuire. "There are some people who impress the world in that way. They really don't have to do things. It is simply known that, when the time comes, they can do great things. I suppose that it is that way with Andrew Chase."

"I'd like to see how much of a hero he is!" said I, bristling at the thought. For were not my knuckles still sore from the thumping which I had given to his brother?

"Perhaps you *will* have a chance to find out what sort of a man he is," said Father McGuire, looking fixedly at me. "But I hope not, my boy. I sincerely hope not!"

"Do you think that I would be afraid of him?" said I, on fire.

He waved a hand as though banishing a question which was not to the point. "However," said he, "I am glad that you were able to handle Harry."

"I did that!" said I, with a great grin of satisfaction. "I wish that you had been there to watch!"

"I wish that I had!" said he, with an apparent warmth of gratification.

"He came off his horse and rushed at me like a mad bull!" said I.

"Weren't you a little afraid?"

"Just for a minute—I was. I'd never stood up to any one who came smashing in like that—as though I were nothing, you see. But even if I was rattled, you had put enough sense into my hands and my arms. They took care of me until I woke up and saw that I could manage this big plunging chap well enough."

"You weren't long in getting your confidence!"

"Not long. I tried him with a few straight lefts—your own brand. Well, father, they went through his guard as if he didn't have one! All I had to do after that was to stand away and keep bobbing his head with my left. You would have thought that his face was tied to my fist by a rubber string, they connected so often!"

I laughed with the brutal joy of that recollection, and Father McGuire was seized with a violent fit of coughing which forced him to cover his face with one hand. When he spoke again, he was looking down at the floor, and not at me.

"But didn't he try to close with you, Lee?"

"He did. But—he wasn't even as strong as I am! Oh, yes, he was strong, and he was pretty hot to kill me, you might say. That made him enough to scare the strength out of most people. But I found after a grip or two that he didn't have much weight on me and that I was really a lot stronger than he. Besides, he didn't know the first thing about wrestling. He didn't know a single grip!"

I laughed again, dropping my head far back and letting

the chuckle shake me to my very toes.

"When you saw that, he was pretty much at your mercy?" said Father McGuire.

"I begged him not to come in after me," said I. "I knew that I could do anything I wanted with him."

"When did you find that out?" asked Father McGuire.

"Oh, before we'd swung our fists more than two or three times."

"But he wouldn't stop?"

"No. He kept coming in. So I gave him a lesson he won't forget! I tried everything you ever taught me, Father McGuire. I tried jabs in close, and straight punches, and half-arm rips and smashes, and overhand dropping punches that went smashing all the way down his face, and uppercuts short and full arm. I hooked and even swung; and then I hit straight. Oh, it was great!

"I did everything but play for his body; I wanted to leave some strength in him to stand up till the finish—but when I heard the sheriff coming, I knew that I couldn't play with Chase any more. So I tried a full-arm smash at him. You know that driving right that you've taught me, with just a bit of hook at the end of it? I gave him that. You'd of thought that I'd hit him on the back of the head with a mallet, the way he dived into the dust! You'd of laughed, Father McGuire!"

Father McGuire jumped suddenly out of his chair and began to walk up and down the room. It was a great thing to see his nervous, quick steps. I felt that he was fighting the battle through again from beginning to end and rejoicing in having such a fine pupil as I.

Suddenly he said to me: "Go harness the horse to the buggy, Leon."

"Is there anything wrong?" said I.

"I'm too much moved to talk to you about it now," said

Father McGuire. "But I want you to go and harness that horse at once. Then bring it around to the front of the house. Hurry, Leon!"

I could see that he was very excited; and what he was excited about had to do with my description of the fight, I had no doubt. However, I knew that it would not be wise to speak to him about it now. I had formed the habit of obedience while I was under his rule.

So I went out to the pasture and called the horse and harnessed it when the good-natured old beast came to my call. In a few minutes I had the buggy and the horse in front of the house. I found that Father McGuire was already waiting at the gate. He climbed into the rig and took the reins.

"Run inside for your hat and your coat," said he.

"Do *I* go with you?" said I.

"You *do*," said he. "But now, hurry as fast as you can! This thing that we have to do must be done together."

I did as he directed, and presently we whirled away down the street, and out of the dingy blackness of Mendez to the open plains, where the stars burned twice as low and twice as bright, with a thousand miles of stillness lying on either hand. We jogged on for five miles, and then Father McGuire turned the horse into the lane that led for the new Chase house!

I could not believe it, at first. I turned in the seat and stared down at the erect, square-shouldered outline of the little priest. How familiar that silhouette was, with the head thrusting a little forward, eagerly!

I began to grow afraid. I could never tell what was passing in that brain of his. I really knew him less at the end of eight months' living with him than I had known him at the beginning. What was his purpose now?

He was sufficiently mysterious to me to make me realize that I must make no question of him; and I also realized that whatever he intended must be right. I could not imagine him doing a wrong thing. However, no boy is entirely interested in "right" for its own sake. The end is the thing that the boy has his attention fastened upon, and he does not particularly care about the means to that end.

We stopped at the hitching rack before the house and I, getting down and taking the hitching rope from the back of the buggy, was lost in wonder at the dimensions of the big building.

I had seen it before, when the Carey family lived here. I had even delivered meat at the door. But Mr. Chase had ordered the remodeling of the place on an extensive scale before he came to take up his residence in it. It was three stories, instead of two, and it soared above me like a mountain. It rambled away on either side in wings, either one of which was larger than the biggest house in little Mendez town. Here and there was a lighted window, dotting the great outline of the big place rather than illuminating it.

Chapter Six

Leon's Apology

We went up to the front door, with Father McGuire walking briskly in the lead; I lagged to the rear, more unwilling with every step that we took. In answer to the bell, a servant opened the door.

"Father McGuire wishes to see Mr. Chase on an important matter," said the little priest.

We were ushered into a lofty hall. It ran to the uppermost roof of the house, and I lifted my eyes with awe up the shadowy walls of that spacious chamber. Then we were led into a little room at the side. I remained standing, and so did Father McGuire, with his eyes bent upon the floor.

Then a brisk, heavy step sounded through the hall, and I saw a florid man with a vivacious eye and a well-trimmed, blond mustache standing before us. He went up to the priest and offered his hand.

"You are Father McGuire?" said he.

"I am," said my friend. "I have come to introduce you to young Leon Porfilo."

He nodded to me.

"This is Mr. Chase, Leon."

"Ah?" said the rancher, and he looked at me with a sudden stiffening of his upper lip, which reminded me of his son's expression as he rushed into battle. "How do you do, Leon Porfilo," said he, without shaking hands.

"What I have to say," said Father McGuire, "I wish to say before all your family, Mr. Chase. I want Mrs. Chase to hear it. I wish to have your elder son present. I particularly wish to have Harry Chase in the room."

The rancher flushed a little and looked not at the priest but straight at me, until I wished myself a thousand miles from that spot. I idled restlessly from foot to foot on the thick rug.

"Harry," said Mr. Chase, "as you probably know, is not presentable this evening."

"Nevertheless," said Father McGuire, "it is very important that he should be one of those to hear what we have to say!"

I was disturbed by the plural. What did *I* have to say? I had not the slightest idea!

"Do you consider it important?" said Mr. Chase, with a cold little sneering smile, which again was familiar to me from my meeting with his son.

"I consider it important—very," said Father McGuire, and his intent eyes drew back the glance of Mr. Chase until the sneer disappeared from his face.

"This is very odd," said the rich man.

"It is very necessary," corrected Father McGuire.

Mr. Chase suddenly snapped his fingers. "You interest me," said he. "You shall have it your own way."

He took us down the hall and into a big living room

where a little lady was tinkling the keys of a big piano.

She was Mrs. Chase, very slender, with a girlish figure and a face still beautiful—as dark in complexion and eyes and hair, as her husband was fair. She shook hands most cordially with Father McGuire, but when she heard my name, she started and gave me a look of horror as though a snake had crawled across her path. Poor lady, if she could have looked a little more deeply into the future, she would have loathed me in very fact!

Then I was presented, with the priest, to the elder son, Andrew. He was like his father in bulk. He was like his mother in the graceful finish of his face and his body, and in his black hair and his dark, bright eyes.

He had a cool, calm way with him that sent a shiver through me.

He said to Father McGuire: "I don't understand why your young friend should be here tonight."

I suppose no one could have thought of a more insulting speech; I wanted to kill him—or to flee from the house! Then I heard Mr. Chase exclaiming: "Andrew! No more of that! We are to have Harry with us, also."

"Harry?" said Andrew, giving me a flashing glance that went through me like a sword blade. "An infernal outrage! Do you want to humiliate the poor boy again?"

However, Mr. Chase sent for Harry; and he talked easily enough through the following heavy pause until Harry appeared with his face crisscrossed with bandages. Only one eye was exposed, and that looked forth through a discolored slit. When he saw me, he stopped short, and then he whirled on his father in a rage.

"Why do you want *me* here, sir?" said he.

Mr. Chase waved to Father McGuire. "You see," said he, "that this makes quite a commotion in my house. I suppose that you have something to say to us, father?"

"I have come," said Father McGuire, "in the first place to apologize for the outrageous thing which my young protégé has done to-day!"

"Come, come," broke in Andrew Chase. "There's no need of apologies! Apologies don't make the thing any better. Harry has simply been thrashed. Words don't help matters!"

"Young man," said the fiery priest, "you speak too quickly about important matters. You lack a quarter of a century of life; when you reach that age you will know better than to speak without forethought. I have come to tell you that there is no cause for Harry Chase to feel any shame."

"That's a rare one," said Andrew.

"If you please, Andrew!" said his father with much dignity.

Father McGuire wheeled on Andrew, saying: "Would you be ashamed of your brother if he had been beaten by a professional pugilist?"

"Of course not."

"What I wish to tell you in the first place is that Leon Porfilo has been practicing boxing under my instruction for the greater part of a year. A match between him and an untrained boy is as bad as a match between a man armed with a rapier and another armed with a paper knife.

"The thing which he has done today, in taking advantage of his skill and his training to batter a boy who probably has never had a moment of scientific training— is simply a frightful outrage. I have come to tell you that I feel this thing. I am covered with shame because of it. I believe that Leon himself realizes that he has done a shameful thing!"

It was quite a staggering position for me, as you may imagine. I felt the very floor shaking beneath my feet, but I felt, also, the burning eyes of Father McGuire upon me. What he had said was a revelation to me. The sudden frankness and the bitter truth of his words rushed in on me. I saw that the thing of which I had been so proud was, in reality, worthy of nothing but a great, black shame.

I managed to make myself take a step or two out in front of Father McGuire. I was trembling and about as sick as any boy has ever been in this world, because a boy's pride is almost his whole soul, his whole existence!

I said in a gasping voice: "I didn't see it that way when we were fighting, Harry. But I see it now. I—I acted like a dog, because I knew more than you did. I want to—beg your pardon."

I wonder if I have felt such a consummate agony as I did at that moment, dragging that apology up from the most exquisitely sensitive roots of my soul.

I think every one was a little astonished and shocked; there was too much shame and pride and suffering in my voice and my face to go as a light thing; and there was a bit of a hush until Andrew Chase said carelessly:

"Well, Harry, there you are. I suppose that makes up for the good beating you got."

"No!" cried Harry. "I'll never stop until I've beaten him worse than he beat me! I'll never stop until he's——"

"Harry!" cried his mother. "What are you saying?"

"I'll never stop," cried Harry, "until I've had him on his knees, begging for mercy—with other people to hear him beg!"

There were exclamations from his father and his mother that half covered these words. But when he was ended, I heard Andrew Chase say with a contented smile:

"That's a very good way to put it, Harry. I love you for that!"

It is one thing to humiliate oneself in order to make an apology. It is another thing to tender the apology and have it refused. I felt a hot burst of emotion against Father McGuire for having brought me into this predicament; what the others had to say I hardly marked, but I heard Father McGuire saying:

"This is an extremely unreasonable attitude, Mr. Chase. I trust that you realize it!"

"In matters of common sense," the proud man answered, "I interfere with the affairs of my sons. In matters of honor, I trust them to find the right way. After all, your young friend admits that he has brought this trouble upon his own head!"

Father McGuire was angered, and he showed it. He said: "My hope now is that no harm will come out of this matter. My meaning by that is: No greater harm than has been done already."

"What may you mean by that?" asked Mr. Chase, frowning.

"If you do not understand now," said Father McGuire, "I trust that the meaning of what I say will never be made clear to you later on."

He bade them good night and took me with him from the house. I was never so glad to leave any place.

On the way home, he gave me the reins.

"She steps out for you better," he explained. "Besides, I'm too angry to trust myself to the handling of a horse."

We had flown down the road at a fast clip for a mile or more and turned onto the main highway before he touched my arm.

"I am proud of you, Leon," said he. "I could not tell you beforehand how you should act at the house of Mr. Chase. I wanted to see if you had enough pride and sense to see what was the right way. I think that you have done enough! More than any other young man of this community would have done. It was a handsome apology, all things considered. It was a handsome apology, after I put you so brutally in the wrong. I think you have done quite enough!"

He repeated these things in this manner for several moments, and I could see that he was highly excited. During the rest of the ride, he broke out from time to time in the same fashion. He would ask me questions which were already answered in his own mind and which therefore required no comment from me.

"If there is evil, now, let it be upon their own heads! We have done enough. We have gone more than half-way!"

Or again he cried suddenly: "Did you notice that handsome rascal, Andrew Chase? Do you understand now why it is that a man does not have to do great things before he is considered a great man?"

I could understand very readily. Little as Andrew had said, I knew him. I felt his steady nerve, his cruel pride, his dauntless courage. When one sees a great locomotive panting and trembling on the rails, one's sense of power is almost as great as though it is seen dragging a great train up a sharp grade.

We reached home, and Father McGuire said no more to me on the subject for a full three weeks. Then he came home one night with a darkened forehead and said:

"Young Harry Chase is taking boxing lessons. Have you heard of that?"

I admitted that I had not.

He went on to tell me that Andrew had cast about for some time looking for a proper instructor. He himself was a fine boxer, as he did all things well. But he wanted a still more expert man to give Harry his tuition. Finally one had been found. He was an ex-pugilist who had made something of a stir in the middleweight ranks until a broken jaw, which refused to knit properly, had made him retire from the ranks of the professional pugilists.

"You understand, Leon, what this means," said Father McGuire, and there he dropped the subject.

But I understood very well, of course. I had a too vivid picture of those two big men struggling together, while the pugilist stood by and corrected their errors— or, rather, the errors of Harry, for it was hard to imagine Andrew Chase doing anything wrong. If he hit, he would by nature strike, and strike hard. If he blocked, he could not fail to pick off the flying hand that shot toward him. How vastly Harry would stride forward in this manner, with a marvelous sparring partner and an excellent teacher every day!

Moreover, the entire district heard of what was happening, and the entire district waited in suspense.

It was considered the height of sporting correctness, among those Westerners. Since I had learned to box, it was thought very fit and proper that Harry Chase should perfect himself as much as possible and then challenge me to a fight fairly and in the open. Had the Chase family been other than upright and fair, it was pointed out that they could have used their enormous influence in many ways to make my life miserable.

I suppose, for my part, that Mr. Chase looked upon this proceeding on the part of his son with as much approval as any one else. He could not see, any more than the others could see, the dreadful results which would eventually roll out of this small beginning. It seemed no more than play, boyish rivalry! But I, in fact, understood vaguely what was coming. Not fully or directly, or I should have fled from the country and taken a new name and gone to hide myself from the tragedy which was coming. But it was only a dim premonition.

Father McGuire had brought home that thought to me by the dark suggestions which were in the speech he had made to the Chase family on the unforgetable night. He called the same forebodings into my mind one day when he said to me:

"Are you still working in the gymnasium, Leon?"

I told him that I was going through my paces every day for a full two hours. He looked at my drawn face and pink cheeks and nodded.

"Yet, Leon," said he, "I think that the wisest thing would be for you to leave this district and go some place else!"

"Run away from Harry Chase!" cried I.

"Not from Harry Chase—but from his brother and from yourself!" said Father McGuire.

I could only gape at him. I could understand that Andrew, in time, might become a menace to me. But what danger lay in my own nature, I could not for the moment see. I was to learn in good time.

But Father McGuire did not stop at good advice. When he saw that my pride was sure to keep me at my task and sure to keep me ready for Harry Chase whenever that strong young man was prepared to tackle me, the priest gave over all talk. He simply made it a point to go out to our little gymnasium with me every day and spar.

Marksmanship in boxing becomes of vital importance, and Father McGuire encouraged my practice by devising a novel idea which, I think, was unique with him. He plastered a bit of tape just in front of the second big knuckle on either hand. Then he marked four targets on the big sand bag, one to correspond with either side of a man's chin, one for the pit of the stomach, one for the spot beneath the heart.

None of those targets—which were merely bits of white tape—were larger than half an inch in diameter. Then the tapes on my hands were blackened and the sand bag was started swinging back and forth rapidly. When I attacked that shifting bag, I was supposed to strike at those targets and land on them and on no other spots.

It would astonish you to hear how often I missed and how seldom I landed accurately. There is a temptation, as every boxer knows, to squint the eyes under the physical strain of striking a blow. I learned to keep my eyes open all the time and watch the work of my hands to the instant they landed. I had to learn, not only to hit to the vital target, but also to hit with all my force. For accuracy is useless without the full punching power behind it.

In the meantime, the weeks turned into months, and still there was no appearance of young Harry Chase in the streets of the little town of Mendez. I understood this, also. He was a headlong fellow, but his brother, Andrew, the controlling genius of the family, had seen the effects of my work upon Harry, and knew that there would have to be great work before Harry was able to face me upon even terms.

The winter passed. The spring came. I was seventeen, and I had filled out to something of my full stature. I weighed, at that time, a little more than a hundred and seventy-five pounds; and though it was all hard, effective weight, my efforts to follow the gyrations of Father McGuire when he boxed with me had kept my footwork light and easy, and my boxing fast and sure.

In the meantime, there was a good deal of talk in Mendez, and most of it was not complimentary to the courage of Harry Chase. He would never be ready for the fight, they said. But I had no doubts on that score. I had seen Andrew Chase, and I knew his power of will. So, on a fine, clear day in the first week of May, I was not surprised when young Sam Harrison came running to Father McGuire's house to tell me that Harry Chase was in the town and asking for me.

Chapter Seven

A Bit of Strategy

I cannot help wondering, often, why they had not arranged to fight this battle in some secluded barn. I suppose it was because Andrew insisted on having the affair fought under conditions of ground and scene which would duplicate the first event. Men and women and boys of Mendez had seen his brother frightfully and shamefully beaten in the first place. He proposed that Harry should beat me with equal violence, in the same place—and with the same number of witnesses.

The same number? The street was alive with people as I walked down its length. Work was stopped. Women crowded the upper windows, and there was a flying cloud of boys, big and small, come out to be on the site of the encounter.

I saw the three of them, finally, as I turned the corner into the old Mexican plaza which was the center of the village. They were coming across the open plot, and I went slowly toward them, very white of face, I am afraid, and very stiff of body. In my stomach there was a feeling of waterish weakness.

There was Andrew Chase, first of all, no taller than his younger brother, and scarcely as bulky, but lifted out from the others as a tiger is distinguishable among mere cattle. At his side was his younger brother, looking drawn and fit for action, and rosy-faced with self-confidence. On the farther side of Harry was a thick-shouldered man with a broad, twisted face. That was Dan Rowley, the prize fighter. I had no need to be told that. I felt, somehow, that although I had to fight one of the trio only, the weight of the brains of the entire three would overwhelm me.

Andrew stepped out before the others. He came up to me and said simply enough: "I suppose you know why Harry is in town?"

I had to gulp down a cold lump in my throat, before I could admit that I did surmise why he had come.

Andrew lingered an instant, with contempt in his eyes as he noted my pallor. Then he turned on his heel and went back to his brother.

He said, loud enough for every member of that densely gathering crowd to hear him: "I don't think you'll have enough work to warm you up, Harry. He's in a blue funk!"

That, if you like, was a cruel speech. It brought upon me an instant focusing of many eyes. Then anxious voices began to mutter behind me:

"Don't lay down to him, kid! He's bigger, but you'll beat him. He can't lick you, Lee!"

He was, in fact, a vital matter of ten or fifteen pounds heavier; and he had that great additional advantage of an extra year. Every year at that young season of life helps to harden and toughen a boy's muscle.

I gave my supporters a wan smile and replied by silently stripping off my coat and then my shirt. I tightened my belt and stood out, naked to the waist. It caused a little murmur of enthusiastic applause. In fact, I was well trained. My chest was already arching as manhood increased upon me; my arms were alive with long, sinewy muscles, and my neck was growing heavier.

That murmur died away entirely when Harry Chase followed my example and showed across the breast and shoulders, beneath a stretched filament of transparent skin, thick, rubbery cushions of muscle, and deep currents of power playing up and down his arms like currents of shifting quicksilver, at every movement of his hands.

I suppose that each of us looked three years older as we squared off. I was grave, thoughtful, and—frankly—very weak with fear. Harry Chase was fairly bursting with a confident sense of his power and of the great new art of self-defense into which he had been initiated so thoroughly.

How thoroughly, I could tell by his manner of looking eagerly into my eyes as he put up his hands, and by the easy, graceful manner in which he came into his guard—nothing rigid in an inch of his big body.

I knew it would be a fight and a real one, this time. But I did not think any too well of my chances. How much I should have given for the kindly, shrewd face of Father McGuire behind me!

The crowd thought no better of me than I did of myself. I looked big and strong, but Harry seemed still larger and still more powerful. Besides, he overmatched me quite with his bubbling confidence and his handsome, smiling face.

"I'll put down fifty bones on Harry Chase!" bellowed a cow-puncher.

"I'll lay you three to one on Chase!"

"Aw, pikers, take a breath! A hundred to twenty on Harry Chase."

It was a veritable roar, and the more they talked the smaller was the chance of their finding a backer for me until a sharp voice cut across them: "I'll take every bet on Chase. I'll take you at your own odds. Here, you, where's that hundred to twenty? Here's my twenty. Here's some more—plenty more for anybody who wants to bet!"

I turned and saw a gray-headed, thin-faced man with a very solemn face, and both hands filled with money. He saw me turn and he said: "I think you can lick that big sucker, kid. Do you think so?"

"I don't know," said I, with a little warming of my blood.

"If you don't know, it's a bad sign," said he in his crisp way. "But remember one thing—the first blood isn't the last blood!"

He was quite right about one part of his speech, at least. First blood went to Harry Chase, and he drew it with his first blow—which was a long-sliding straight left that would have made Father McGuire shout with admiration. It darted over my tardy, feeble guard as we squared off, and it landed fairly on the end of my nose, with a tingling force that snapped my head back and brought the warm blood. My nose had turned numb, but I could taste my own blood on my lips.

"Follow up!" cried Andrew Chase. "In at him, Harry! The body!"

That was a very neat bit of strategy—to drive at my body while I was a bit off balance. But the sound of Andrew's voice roused me to desperation. The hands of big Harry were enough against me. The wits of Andrew Chase were a frightful handicap. Like a cornered rat, I opened my eyes and began to fight as if for my life.

I caught two smashing blows by jerking out my elbows, and I saw the face of Harry wither with pain as his hands landed on the sharp bones.

Then I went in with my first attack. But my fighting spirit still was not up, and his skill was immensely improved. I merely found myself hammering at forearms on which my punches landed; then a darting right caught me at the base of the jaw and knocked me staggering.

There was no pause. Harry Chase would not wait for new and easy chances. He followed up every advantage with a lunge like a bull. Plainly that wise brother of his had not attempted to remake the nature of Harry, but had simply added skill to his natural disposition to attack, and still attack, savagely, relentlessly. Harry came swarming after me, and I tried my first trick, which was to lean forward and wrap my arms around my head.

"He's quitting!" screamed a dozen disgusted voices. "He's got enough."

Harry Chase, gasping with a savage joy, hammered at my well-protected head, unheeding the wise shouts of his brother to straighten me up with an uppercut. When both of Harry's hands were flung wide in the eager fury of his assault, I uncovered suddenly and took Andrew's advice myself by snapping my right fist up under the chin of Harry.

Oh, wise Father McGuire! That sharpshooting practice stood me in good stead now. It was not a tremendously powerful blow, but it landed so neatly on the button that Harry Chase reeled away. I slid in after him, brought his guard down with a long blow to the body, and then dropped him in his tracks with a neat right cross that hummed over to the point of the chin.

I stood back in the midst of a wild turmoil; but all I saw was not the fallen fellow on the ground, but the face of Andrew Chase, cold with anger as he fixed his black eyes upon me.

"Take your time, Harry," said Andrew, still with his eyes fixed grimly upon me. "This is a finish fight, and there's no referee to count you out. Take your time and get up when your head has cleared."

The answer of Harry was a roar of fury, and he bounded to his feet to charge again.

Not the blind charges of our first fight. He fought with a wicked skill, in spite of his passion. But still, anger is a cloudy emotion. It dimmed the eyes of Chase, and my own were wide open. I caught him with two long, raking punches as he came in and then, ducking his swings, I opened on his body.

Brave and strong as he was, that fire weakened him and sent him back, gasping. My work was written upon his ribs in crimson splotches, and all around me was an uproar as the backers of Harry strove to hedge their bets.

He charged again, and for the first time I met him with all my might. It was only a left-hander, but that hook spatted against his mouth and laid him flat on his back.

I knew, with a feeling of a strange relief, rather than a great leap of the spirit, that this fight was in my hands, as the first one had been.

Before he was up, I said to Andrew Chase: "He can't hurt me, and I can hurt him. Will you take him off?"

"He'll tear you in two, in a moment," said Andrew, and he was white with a torment of shame and crushed pride. This was his own brother, his own flesh, that was going down before me. He could not forget it; in fact, he never did.

But Harry did not tear me in two.

As he came up: "Stand off and box!" commanded Andrew.

Harry obeyed and stood off to box at long range. It was no use. That was not his natural style. If I could get my gloves past the skillful guard of Father McGuire, I could certainly flash my bare fists past the arms of Harry Chase. I did. His hair leaped on his head as my blows thudded home.

I turned him halfway round with an overhand right that made his knees sag, and the dazed look in his eyes was reflected sharply by a look of anguish and almost terror in the eyes of Andrew.

"Clinch!" shouted Andrew, and poor Harry swung about and lurched in to obey orders.

The habit of obedience to that voice, built of a life of custom, reached even his punch-dazed brain. I let him come in, and then tied up his arms in a clinch—which is a neat little art in itself.

I said over his shoulder: "You fellows see that Harry Chase isn't good enough to lick me. Will you stop this fight before I have to hurt him?"

Andrew stepped forward.

"Have you had enough of this, Porfilo?" said he.

"I? No, he's hardly touched me."

"The yellow comes out on a greaser sooner or later," said Andrew, sneering. "I thought it might be coming out in you!"

It was about as nasty a speech as anyone could have devised, and it was greeted with a heavy silence from the circle around me. I let Harry Chase tear himself away from me. There was a devil in me then. I caught poor Harry with two cutting blows to the face that brought a gush of crimson each time.

"Has he had enough?" I shouted to Andrew Chase.

"You cur!" breathed Andrew Chase. "You'll be ripe for me, one of these days!"

Again his speech was greeted with silence. As for me, I was beginning to see red in my rage. I slashed Harry across the face again, and as he staggered, I plunged my right hand into the pit of his stomach. He doubled up and fell with a grunt. There he lay, kicking and squirming in the dust, quite winded. I stepped across his fallen body and said to Andrew Chase:

"You called me a greaser, Chase. Do you mean that?"

"Are you ashamed of your race?" sneered he.

"You're older and stronger than I am," said I, "but I won't stand for that."

"What will you do about it, then, Porfilo?" said he.

"I'll have your apology," said I, beginning to tremble.

"My apology?" said he, and smiled.

I struck out that smile by flicking my open hand across his face, and the next instant a thunderbolt struck me to the ground.

It was the fist of Andrew Chase. I had heard of blinding speed before, but this was as inescapable as the lightning flash to which I have compared it. The blow landed fairly on my chin; I felt a concussion at the base of my head; and I dropped into deep darkness.

When I recovered, there was still a spinning blackness before my eyes. In the swirl I detected many faces, and I struggled to my feet, when I staggered dizzily.

"Where's Andrew Chase?" I asked.

But Andrew Chase was gone. He had left and taken his brother with him long before I recovered from the trance into which his fist had knocked me.

Now, as my head cleared, and as I realized what had happened, I found strained, stern faces around me and many eyes that looked upon me with a sort of intense hatred. But that hatred was not for me. It was for the thing which I had been forced to suffer. I saw the lean, gray-headed man come through the rest, and he took my hand.

"It was a low thing," said he. "How old are you, my friend?"

"Seventeen," said I.

He turned and spat in the dust. "He's seventeen!" said he to the others.

They nodded their confirmation.

"How old is Andrew Chase?" he asked.

"Twenty-two," said several voices.

"A grown man and a boy," said the little stranger. "Do you allow this thing to pass like this? Is that the Arizona way?"

"I don't want help," said I. "I'll handle my own affairs. Andrew Chase is too much for me now, but I'm not at my full strength, yet."

The little man turned his gray head to me again. "If I'm not mistaken," said he, "there'll be a little nest of hell raised around this town as a memento of today. The rest of you can write down what I say. Keep it in mind. Keep it in red. Some day a bomb will break. Then I should not like to be in the boots of the Chase family!"

That black day was not relieved by the homecoming of Father McGuire, who found me with my books spread out before me on the library table and my head buried in my hands. He sat down opposite me. I was too sick at heart to look up at him.

"Of course," said he, "I have heard everything."

I did not answer.

He went on: "I made a point of asking from several eyewitnesses. Each of them gave me a picture that was a little blacker that the one before. Personally, I cannot understand it! Andrew Chase is not the sort of a man who could do such a thing. It isn't possible. It isn't in his eyes or his speech. I can't imagine it in his heart."

Still I did not speak.

"Have you made up your mind about what you will do, Leon?" said he at the last.

"I'll wait," said I bitterly. "It's all that I *can* do, isn't it?"

He sighed.

"Is it too much to ask you to forget?" said he.

At this, I looked up indeed! I smiled at him. "It's too much!" said I. "A hundred people saw him do it, and they'll never forget. How can you ask me to?"

Father McGuire rose and walked restlessly around the room, striking his hands together and then dragging them apart.

"The thing grows," said he. "It grows every moment! I had a foreboding of it before, but now I feel the certainty of it. The pride of Andrew Chase—that's the keystone of the arch! It will never stop working until he has ruined everything! How many lives will be involved?"

Chapter Eight

A Proposition

I have no doubt that, had it been any person other than
Andrew Chase, the community would have taken action,
and very stern action, against him. But he was the son of
the richest and most respected man in the whole range;
and he was also Andrew Chase! To see him, to conceive
of him, was to conceive and see a person incapable of
a small or knavish action. He might be capable of some
crime, but it would have to be upon a grand scale. But
Andrew Chase in the role of a bully? Surely not!

I myself, thinking of the matter, could hardly see him
again doing the very thing which the purple lump on
my chin was evidence that he had done. He might be a
thousand things—but surely never a bully!

I do not believe that it was the pressure of any public
opinion, which made him do what he next attempted.
The thing came out of his own mind and his own heart,
and I suppose that I have to admit that it was worthy

of him. The hatred which I feel now for Andrew was built up in after years. He had changed from his youth before he accomplished the things which make me loathe him now!

At any rate, that same evening, as we were finishing our coffee after supper, old Mimsy answered the doorbell and came scurrying back in a fright to tell us that Mr. Andrew Chase had just arrived to call upon us.

Father McGuire gave me a look which was eloquent enough. But I told him that I would do nothing foolish, and that I hoped I would not say a foolish thing, either. Then we went in together to Andrew Chase. Mimsy had ushered him into the library. He stood up to greet us as we entered.

First he shook the hand of Father McGuire. Then he turned to me and said: "I won't offer you my hand at present, Porfilo. Not until we have had a chance to talk and you have had a chance to consider my apology. Then we will shake hands, I hope."

Father McGuire fairly groaned with relief.

He said: "I knew that you would do something like this. It was unlike you to take advantage of him, Andrew Chase. I am grateful to Heaven for it."

"It was the most detestable thing I have done in my life," said Andrew. "I am grateful to you because you knew I could not let things stand as they were without another word. Of course I have to do something. I am just now turning over in my mind some sort of an apology which may please Leon Porfilo. Do you know exactly what I did to him?"

This was really exceedingly adroit. He turned to Father McGuire and discussed his own sins as though it were a detached wickedness with which he really had no vital connection. Even at that age I was able to understand and admire his policy.

"I think that I have heard all the details of the affair," said Father McGuire, "but not from Leon."

"Exactly," said Andrew, flashing a quick glance at me. "A man of spirit doesn't talk about such things, of course. Well, sir, to put the whole thing in a word, Leon Porfilo, who is a gentleman, was used by me as though he were a rat. That's putting it mildly. In the first place, I called him a greaser.

"In the second place, I stood to what I said. In the third place, when he very promptly and properly resented what I had said, I took advantage of my superior age and strength to knock him senseless. I tell you, sir, that when I review those things, I cannot see myself in the role. There must have been a devil in me!"

He had grown red and then pale, and there was a look of disgust in his handsome face.

"I've done such a thing," said he, "as a man cannot forget. It will be a detestable stain in my mind so long as I live. There is only one extenuating remark which I can make. I don't claim it as an excuse, but to help to show you how I could have acted as I did act: I was maddened at the sight of my brother battered and helpless in the hands of a younger and smaller man than himself after all the work which we had put upon him to make him capable of a better fight! I was in a frenzy, and the thing got the best of me. It was worse than drunkenness; it was a thing that makes me writhe now as I think of it!"

"You are very severe with yourself," said Father McGuire gravely. "But I admit that I feel you are not too severe."

"Not a whit!" declared Andrew Chase.

Here he turned sharply round upon me. "Porfilo," said he, "I have several direct apologies to make to you.

"In the first place, I reflected upon an ancestry which is just as cleanly Anglo-Saxon as my own.

"In the second place, I badgered you while you were in the midst of the fight with another man who should have given you hard work enough without my help.

"In the third place, like a brutal bully, I took advantage of my own size and my strength to strike you down."

He concluded this list of facts, which made my face burn, by saying simply: "If a man had done such things to me, I think I could never forget it. I tell you that frankly. But that is because my family has always been cursed with a species of false pride which is one of the worst vices in the world.

"I would nourish a sulky resentment until I had a chance to fight it out. But I think there may be finer stuff than that in you, Porfilo. If you accept my apology in the first place, don't dream that anyone will ever accuse you of cowardice. Not at all! The manner in which you have disposed of my brother on two successive occasions——"

Here he was forced to pause, for he was breathing hard, and his breath came in gasps. The color changed in his face, and for a moment he was livid. He mastered himself as quickly as he could, but I had had a sufficient glimpse of emotions which were almost beyond my conception. Proud I might be, but I could never rival such pride as this, which became a veritable physical thing!

"In a word," went on Andrew Chase, "I am offering you my hand. If you take it, I shall feel that you have helped to clean away a very soiled place in my honor. Will you be generous enough to forgive me for the things I have done, Porfilo?"

He said it in an indescribable manner, so filled with grace and with directness, so filled with humility and with pride that my heart melted at once. Truly, this fellow was full of magic! I had been raging with resentment an instant before. Now I found myself surging with the very kindest emotions concerning Andrew Chase.

"Why," I said, "I can understand. You wanted Harry to win. Then you got mad—and you did a lot of things that anybody might be apt to do. I won't keep any resentment. If you knocked me down, you did it fairly enough. Some day I might want to take another shot at you, though."

"When you do," said he, very grave, "come to me day or night and we'll go off by ourselves or back to the same town plaza, and you can have your satisfaction. A large satisfaction it's apt to be, if you grow into your promise for manhood, Leon!"

Was not this enough? Yes, sufficient to make me seize his hand and to wring it with all my might.

"I've forgotten everything—I—I thank you for being so square and coming to me like this. Tomorrow I'm going to let people know that I have no grudge against you!"

"Will you do that?" he asked a little eagerly.

"I will."

"Then we can talk about the next thing that's in my mind, and in my father's mind, also. It's really more difficult than the first proposition. I may need your help in it, Father McGuire!"

"You've done one good thing to-night," said Father McGuire. His heart was in his voice. "It'll be odd if I don't help you to do another."

"This has to do with poor Harry. I told you before that the Chase family is cursed with a devilish pride, and Harry, poor fellow, has as big a share as any of us. Well, Father McGuire, he has tried twice to match his fists against Leon's and twice he has been beaten fairly and squarely by a youngster smaller and younger than himself. Both times a whole town has been able to look on at the affair! That's rather irksome, you'll admit."

"I admit it," said Father McGuire, as grave as ever.

"Harry knows, now, that he hasn't the hand craft to stand up to Leon Porfilo. Very few men of any age *could*. But most men would accept that fact, no matter how they had to grit their teeth about it. My great fear is that Harry is apt to go a step farther. I am afraid, in a word, that he may take to some other weapon than his hands!"

Neither Father McGuire nor I spoke a word in answer to this.

Andrew Chase went on: "We can't control Harry. He's half insane with shame and rage. If we send him away, he'll slip back and come at you. Then Heaven knows what the consequences may be. He's a handy fellow with a gun; far handier than he is with his fists! But I don't think fear of him would ever budge you, Leon.

"What we want to do—my father and I—is to ask you to slip out to a different section of the country. For instance, if you had in mind something such as starting in partnership with some older man—say the cattle business, or a long apprenticeship, or some such matter—why, if five or six thousand in spot cash would influence you— it would be a delight to supply you!"

Father McGuire looked at me, and I at him. I was bewildered. Then the priest put his hand on my shoulder.

"I have had only one son in my house, Mr. Chase," said he.

"I believe I understand," said Andrew gently, "and therefore I know that you will not stand between him and a bright future. Besides, you would be helping my family out of a frightful danger."

"I think that is true," said Father McGuire. He made a little pause before he turned to me. Their eyes bore heavily upon me.

"My dear Leon," said that good man, "it goes much against my heart, but I feel that for your own sake and also for the sake of that headstrong young man, Harry Chase, you should accept what Mr. Chase has suggested. Take time, then, before you give me an answer!"

I did take time. I turned that matter back and forth as deliberately as I could, but, strive as I would, I could not reconcile myself to the idea. It was one thing to accept the apology of Andrew Chase and continue to live on as I had been living before in the house of good Father McGuire. It was still another matter to advance against the public voice by leaving Mendez and skulking away so secretly that Harry Chase might never find me.

No matter how many times a man proves himself a hero, if he has ever shown the white feather, even for a fraction of a second, it is neither forgotten nor forgiven. So it would be with my name and my fame.

I looked up from all of these reflections straight into the eye of Andrew Chase.

"I respect you too much," I told him, "to think that you'd advise me to do this, if you'd looked at it from my angle. I can't back out. I've got to stay here and see this through."

Andrew Chase turned with a gesture of despair to Father McGuire.

But I stopped all argument and killed it at the root by simply saying: "Twenty years from now, suppose somebody from Mendez met me and said to himself: 'There goes the fellow that was scared out of Mendez by young Harry Chase!' Well, that would be enough to make me wish that I'd died."

Of course, being sensible men, they knew that they could not argue against pride and prejudice like this. They simply glanced at one another, Andrew with his question and Father McGuire with a shake of the head. Then Andrew changed his tone at once. He told me he was sorry that he could not move me to do what he and his father wanted me to, but at the same time that did not alter his respect and liking for me.

He shook my hand again, asked me again to forgive him, and was assured by my simple self that I was glad to have met him, even at a price such as I had paid.

When Andrew had left, Father McGuire said: "Did you mean that?"

"I meant it!" said I. "Of course, some day I'm going to try to thrash him, because of the way he knocked me down. But——"

"Don't you suppose that he knows that?" said Father McGuire. "Haven't you told him that?"

"Of course!" I admitted.

"Do you think that he'll stand by and let you have that chance?"

"A man like Andrew Chase will," said I.

"I don't know," said Father McGuire. "But, between you and me, I think this young man talks just a little too smoothly. He's only twenty-two, and though that may seem a very mature age to you, it makes me wonder! He controls himself too well. There is a great deal of the diplomat about young Mr. Chase, or else I am very mistaken."

I gave no credit to Father McGuire's insinuations of double dealing on the part of Andrew. I was only seventeen!

A new phase of my life began to develop now. By the warning of Andrew Chase himself, we knew that

Harry was more or less of an expert with a revolver, and since he was such an expert, I expected him daily to ride down upon me and attempt to gain his satisfaction at my expense by putting a bullet through my head.

For my part, I suppose that I had handled weapons more than most youngsters. I had done more than my share of hunting, and I was a good hand with a rifle. With a revolver I had done my share, too, of blazing away at snakes or rabbits that crossed my path, and wasted my ten or twenty bullets for every target I struck.

But now I began to work feverishly in preparation for the struggle which must lie ahead—according to the warning from Andrew himself. I bought a brand-new Colt and a large stock of ammunition. Every day, I took a new horse, which I had bought—a strong-limbed mustang well able to support my weight—and galloped off to a secluded spot between two hills on the desert. There I hammered away at some difficult target in all manner of difficult positions on horseback and on foot.

Every morning I went out for at least an hour; every afternoon I was away again. Sometimes I went out in the gray of the evening. For who could tell under what light conditions I might have to meet Harry Chase?

Three months, four months, and there was no sign of Harry Chase. He had gone from the vicinity of Mendez. His family had sent him, it appeared at last, not to an Eastern school, but far across the water to England. Not for English culture, but for English safety.

I felt that I was rescued from the most vital pressure of danger, but still, all through the winter and into the dawn of my eighteenth year the next spring, I was working hard and faithfully with my revolver, and with the gloves of Father McGuire.

My lessons did not greatly suffer. When a young man is keyed up for one piece of work, he is apt to be able to do all of his work much more effectively. So it was with me. All the progress I had made in my first two years of study was not half of what I advanced through in my third year under Father McGuire.

You will wonder what his attitude may have been toward my constant practice with guns. It was rather amusing, but very characteristic.

"You used to fight all the time, before you learned how to box, Lee. Since you learned to box, you've fought only three times—twice with Harry Chase and once with Andrew."

I turned a dark red, at this. The mention of my "fight" with Andrew always touched a tender spot in my nature.

"When a man knows what a blow is and how it *should* be struck," went on Father McGuire, "he is not so apt to be a quarrelsome chap. You must not think that most of the battles on the frontier were the work of real gunmen, either. There are a few men who fight because they do love bloodshed. There are a few unfortunate souls who have that blood lust. But they are very few.

"Most of the men who understand what they can accomplish with a gun in the hand, usually prefer to keep that gun in a holster—until their backs are against the wall. Do you understand me? But the great using up of ammunition, the smashing of windows and mirrors, the ripping up of floors and ceilings—and the occasional slaughter of one another—all of that was the work of the tenderfoot, my boy.

"You wonder why the Westerner doesn't like the tenderfoot? Because he is the chap who makes the trouble! He doesn't know one end of a gun from another. But because he has bought a Colt, he thinks that he will have to use it.

"As for you, Leon, I think that you will not be a fool. I think that this practice will give you better common sense than you ever had before. It will make you respect the possibilities of weapons—in the other fellow's hand as well as in your own!"

This was the philosophy of Father McGuire. I think that the event would have justified the thought of that good man. But I ask you to remember that I was only eighteen; and I think I can show you that the temptation was very great indeed!

At any rate, I take you with me to a certain evening when we sat sleepily over our books in the library of Father McGuire, and I heard a tap at the front door.

I got up to answer it. I remember stumbling over the little rug in front of the library door, and how Father McGuire said testily:

"Your feet, Leon! Your feet! Will you watch your way, my boy?"

I closed the door behind me, went down the hall, and opened the front door. It let in a rush of warm spring wind, and there was Harry Chase standing before me!

Chapter Nine

Stigma

Porfilo," said he, "I'm very late, but I'm here at last."

"I don't know what you mean," said I, nevertheless, understanding very well.

"Think it over a moment," said Harry Chase. "You have disgraced me and beaten me twice. I've come back to fight you in another way."

It seemed incredible. In spite of all that Andrew Chase had told me, still I could not believe the thing!

I said: "Chase, I never struck you unfairly except that in the first fight I took advantage of what I had learned about boxing. But that's not really so very unfair. I apologized for that; I would apologize for it again, if that would make you feel any better!"

He merely sneered at me. "Do you wear a gun?" said he.

"Good heavens," I cried, "do you mean it?"

"Not so loud," said he, glancing sharply over his shoulder. "Not so loud, Porfilo. The priest might hear. I don't want his noise and his chatter. Have you a gun, I asked you?"

"Are you drunk?" I groaned.

"Drunk?" said he, with that same sneering smile which he and his brother understood so well how to use. "I've slipped away from my school on a good excuse and come five thousand miles to see you. I'm supposed to be in Scotland shooting. Instead, I'm here in Arizona—but I intend to have my shooting, all the same. If you're not armed, I have a gun for you. Come outside!"

"I'll have nothing to do with you!" said I, in a real panic, and I started to close the door.

He put his foot against it and caught my arm at the same time.

"Now listen to me," said he. "If you won't fight, I'll make the entire range laugh at you for a coward. I'll publish it everywhere. I'll make the children point their fingers at you! Do you believe me?"

I stepped through the door and stood with him in the night. I was half minded to try the weight of my fists on him now. It would have been an excellent thing if I had. But he had stirred up my pride, and pride in a young man is a tiger.

"Very well," said he. "I'm glad to see that you are reasonable. Have you a gun?"

"No."

"Here is a new Colt. It's loaded in all six chambers. Does it satisfy you?"

I broke it open. I even extracted a shell to see that they were honest stuff. Then I looked up to Chase.

He was smiling his contempt at my open suspicions.

"Very well," said I. "I'm ready."

"Good!" said he.

"How do you want to go about it?"

"I've thought of a way. Come back with me so that we can't be seen from the street."

He led the way to the rear of the house. He took his place at one side of the vegetable patch and I at the other side. I think there were about twenty paces between us, though the distance seemed greater, because we had only starlight.

He said: "It is nearly nine o'clock, and when the first bell strikes, we fire."

"Very well," said I, and freshened my grip on the gun butt.

I can hardly believe this, as I write it down. It seems entirely too blunt and matter of fact to have been the truth. But I am putting down exactly what Harry said and what I answered. If you wish to know what I felt, as I faced him in the dimness, I can only say that I had pushed fear behind me and kept a tight grip on my courage.

I felt, every instant, that terror was about to leap on me and make a trembling woman of me; but still I kept around the corner from such a disaster.

He went on, after a moment: "I am going to kill you, Porfilo, I think. If you have any messages to leave behind you, tell me what they are."

I said: "If I die, there is only one message: Tell Father McGuire that it was a fair fight. Tell him that I'm sorry he didn't guess better. He'll understand what I mean."

"That's fair enough," said Harry Chase.

"I'll offer you the same thing," said I.

He laughed softly. "There's no danger that I'll need a messenger. I'll do my own talking after this affair, Porfilo. When my character has been cleaned up by putting you away, I'll do my own talking. I think it's nearly nine o'clock, Porfilo. Are you ready?"

"I'm ready," said I.

At that instant I heard the old town clock beginning to buzz; a moment later the first note of the bell struck sharply against our ears, and Harry twitched up his gun and fired from the hip. The bullet was well intended. It shaved past my head and clipped away a bit of my red hair at the temple.

My own shot was delayed until I had stretched out my arm, for I knew nothing of these snap shots from the hip. His second shot and my first one rang out at the same instant. His whisked under the pit of my arm, barely grazing my coat on the left side of my body. Mine dropped him in his tracks.

I ran to him while the scream of old Mimsy came shrilling out from her open window. The poor woman had been sitting there in the dark of her room looking out on the night, and she had seen the whole thing, but what our standing opposite one another meant, she had not been able to guess. I suppose her dim eyes did not see the guns in our hands.

I found Harry Chase swearing fluently.

"I've spoiled everything," said he. "That infernal bullet of yours went right through my left thigh. There's nothing to it except a long stay in bed; and a lot of talk at home and in the town. You've won again, Porfilo. But how in Heaven's name I could have missed you—when I've smashed a target an inch square at the same distance—I can't tell! It looks like fate!"

Harry Chase had told the exact truth about his wound. When Father McGuire came running out to us and we had carried Harry into the house, we found by cutting away the trousers that the bullet had pierced the thigh and clipped cleanly through it, leaving a small puncture in front and not an over-large one in the rear of the leg. It was bleeding freely.

Harry Chase caught my arm and said to me in a tensed expression: "Did you shoot low on purpose, Leon?"

"I shot to kill!" I admitted, "because I knew you were shooting to kill me!"

"I was," said he. "You can be the witness, Father McGuire, that I started all this trouble! Leon is not to blame!"

Father McGuire said nothing. He had sent Mimsy away for the doctor. In the meantime, he stopped the flow of blood.

Andrew Chase came in response to our message to him. He came in a matter-of-fact way, shook hands with Father McGuire and with me, and made a remark on the weather. Then something to the effect that Harry would learn, sooner or later, that Porfilo was not meant by Providence to be his meat! It was a very cool speech, and Father McGuire was thoroughly angered. But he said nothing.

"After all," said Andrew calmly to me, "I see that you were wise in not clearing out of the town on account of Harry. It seems that he isn't able to accomplish a great deal—even with a gun!"

I saw that beneath the surface, Andrew was fairly writhing with shame and with contempt for Harry; I saw, too, that he was hating me with all his heart. It was not so much that he wished Harry to win as that he wished him not to lose. A stigma was thrown upon the entire Chase family, it seemed. Or at least, that was his way of looking at it.

They took Harry away in a stretcher and put him in a buckboard because he insisted on being moved. He said cheerfully to Father McGuire:

"I know you'd take care of me, but your food would choke me, after I've tried to punch a bullet through Leon Porfilo like this!"

In this very casual manner, the whole thing ended, for the moment. There were other moments to come. But what astonishes me as I look back on that evening, is the almost humdrum manner in which everything passed off. Even Father McGuire had nothing to say in the way of reproof or advice for the future.

He merely said in his gentle way: "This is the third time with Harry Chase. I think he may have his lesson, now!"

I thought so, too. By this time I was pretty thoroughly convinced that Harry Chase could never put me down, by hand, knife, or gun.

Most naturally, from that moment, I kept my eye upon the house of Chase, because I expected, and Father McGuire expected, that the next move must come from them. They had played all the leading cards so far, and though I had managed to take all the tricks, it was reasonable to suppose that the next disturbance would have a member of the Chase family in it.

I was wrong. The next trouble arose, apparently, from the entrance into Mendez of the most distinguished liar and rascal who ever rode a horse or wore a gun.

I refer to none other than "Turk" Niginski.

No one had so much as heard of Turk Niginski until the day of his arrival. He looked like a Turk, I must confess. He had a pair of bristling mustaches—not many hairs, but long stiff ones that curved down around the corners of his mouth like so many dark scimitars. He had rather slant eyes, very black, with yellow-stained whites. He had a sallow, greasy, shiny skin. His appearance was finished and set off, at once, by a line of ragged-edged, yellow teeth which showed when he grinned. He was always grinning.

This undecorative devil appeared in Mendez and in my life on the same day. I was working in the vegetable garden, preparing a bed for new soil, but excavating it a foot and a half deep, to make room for fresh dirt and dressing.

A voice sang out: "That's him!"

I looked up into the face of the sheriff, who sat his horse beside the fence. With him was Turk Niginski.

I said: "What's wrong?"

The sheriff replied: "Something a good deal worse than anything I've ever had against you before, Lee!"

That alarmed me. Because I knew that I was not liked by the sheriff. He had an inborn, natural suspicion of fighting men, and I had fought and fought and fought through my entire life, as far back as he could remember me. Only with my fists, to be sure, until very lately. But the sheriff had always expected me to really run amuck some day, and the affair with Harry Chase had simply convinced him that his forebodings about me were bound to be accomplished.

He who fights must eventually do a murder! Such was the reasoning of the sheriff. But he was such a wonderfully fair man, such an able and careful sifter of evidence, that I never had a doubt of good treatment at his hands.

"I'll tell you what I've heard," said the sheriff, looking me grimly in the eye. "I've heard that Niginski tried to bum a dollar from you an hour ago. I hear that you kicked him off the place, and when he tried to fight back, you shoved a gun in his face and told him to get off the place."

I was so amazed that I suppose I turned color. Let no one believe the old gag that innocence has a voice of its own. The mere suspicion of guilt, the mere accusation, is enough to throw most men off their feed, as the saying goes. I was thoroughly thrown off by what the sheriff had to say, you may be sure! Consider that I had never so much as seen this Turk before that moment.

The sheriff went on: "He says that you went on and told him that you didn't like the look of him. That the best thing for him to do was to keep right on moving until he was clear out of the town. Because if you seen him again, you was apt to salt him away with a morsel or two of lead. Well, kid, what about it?"

"Sheriff," said I, "I dunno what to say!"

There was innocence for you; but it made such an impression on the sheriff, this innocence of mine, that he scowled blackly upon me.

"Now look me in the eye, kid, and get me right," said he. "I ain't takin' nothin' for granted. It may be that Niginski faked all of this, and that there ain't a word of truth in what he says, though it would be a considerable bit of brain work for a bird with a mug like his."

Truly the face of Niginski seemed one to which a real thought could never come.

"That's exactly what's happened!" I declared with much heat.

"All right," drawled the sheriff. "It may be that you ain't puffed up because you knocked over the Chase kid a few weeks back. It may be that you ain't always been a trouble hunter ever since you was a little kid. It may be that you're all right, and Turk Niginski is all wrong. But I'll tell you pronto, and I'll tell you plain that it looks bad to me. In case you get any wrong ideas to start with, I want you to know that *I'm* runnin' this here town. When it comes to orderin' gents to move along, I'm gonna do all the talkin' that's talked!"

I broke in: "Sheriff, you're not fair!"

He raised his hand and shut me off. "All right, all right!" said he. "You're a saint, maybe. You never done nothin' wrong in all your life. But I tell you that I ain't gonna have this poor saphead scared of his life while he's in Mendez, and if anything happens to him while he's here, I'm gonna come right to you and ask you how come! That's all I got to say!"

He rode away at the side of Turk Niginski, who was grinning in perfect content. I went on blindly with my work, wishing the mysterious liar, Niginski, in the lowest part of the nether regions, to say nothing of the unhappy future which I desired for the sheriff.

But, after a time, I could think of nothing except what might be behind the lie of Niginski. I had never seen this man before. I could never have wronged him. What could be his ultimate intention? My brain came into such a tangle with the idea, that at last I decided to saddle my horse and take a ride in the hope that the wind of a good gallop would blow away the cobwebs.

So I saddled and mounted and whirled out of Mendez on the road north in the direction of the great, cool, cloudy blue mountains which tumbled above the horizon there. My great wish at that moment was that I could break away from Mendez and all of the people in it, and keep straight on with a tireless horse until I was in the upper slopes of those piled summits.

In the midst of these reflections, I looked over my shoulder at the sound of hoofs and saw none other than Turk Niginski rushing up behind me with the ragged mane of his horse wagging high in the wind of his gallop.

I knew there was trouble coming now, in very fact. Turk Niginski had out a gun as he spurred along, and now he raised it and knocked my hat from my head with his first shot—a very capable performance for a man riding at high speed. He was much closer when I put in my bullet in answer. It passed directly through his head, and Niginski lunging from the saddle a limp hulk, struck the knees of my horse and then, rebounding, rolled limp in the dust of the road.

I did not waste time. I knew that the man was dead, and I spurred back to town as hard as I could ride. I went straight to the sheriff, and he seemed to read my story in my excited face.

"Has bad luck come the way of Niginski?" he asked.

"I was riding down the road, harming no one, God be my witness—when I heard the sound of a horse——"

The sheriff finished for me, in a dry voice: "It was Niginski, riding you down with a drawn gun, I suppose. And you had to turn and drop him?"

"Exactly," said I, rather weakly.

"A fine story," said the sheriff, more crisp than ever.

"I can show you my proof. Here is my hat," said I, having scooped it up as I started back for town.

I showed him the bullet hole through it, from front to back.

"Let me see your gun," said the sheriff.

I showed it to him. "Two empty chambers," said he. "Did you have to shoot at him twice?"

I was covered with a very convincing pallor, I have no doubt, for I can remember the cold feel of my face. I could remember now, that after my target practice of the day before, having cleaned my gun thoroughly and reloaded, I had tried a flying shot at a darting jack rabbit that crossed my trail—and missed, of course. Nothing but luck can hit a jack rabbit when it is making its first burst of speed.

"I fired that shot yesterday," said I.

"At what?" snapped out the sheriff.

"A rabbit," said I, more faintly than ever.

The sheriff spat in his disgust. "You come with me," said he, and led me straight to a cell.

There I stayed unheeded for three hours. My first visitor was Father McGuire, who came with a weary face. His voice trembled as he said: "What could have made you do it, Leon? How could that poor man have wronged you in any way?"

That showed me more clearly than anything else could have done how black my situation was. I did not try to explain to Father McGuire. I knew that I would only be able to stumble and halt through my story. So I kept my silence. Thereby I damned myself in the eyes of my only friend.

Everything turned out worse than I could have suspected. Niginski had been found by the road; but his gun, with the emptied chamber, had not been found.

The gun was gone, and thereby the case against me was automatically made perfect. As for my motive in the crime, the townsmen were willing to consider that killing as the natural outcome of a life of violence. It was a natural following-up of the shooting of Harry Chase, no matter how much Harry might have been to blame. The general opinion of everyone was that I should be put away for a good long term.

Chapter Ten

Jailed

Things would have gone better for me in many Western communities, I very well knew. But the reign of law and order which our good sheriff had established in Mendez was such an iron-clad thing that shooting affairs were a novelty. People had been horrified by my affair with Harry Chase; and though Harry was more blamed, still I was blamed, also.

I would not have accepted his invitation to a gun fight, it was felt, unless I had been a lover of gun play. Also, as I have said before, my past record and all my fist work were against me.

Father McGuire believed my tale even less than others might have believed it. He came to see me twice every day. On the second occasion he begged me for a long time to confess and meet my sentence like a man. But I would not make an answer except to say, doggedly, that I was not guilty of any crime. At this, he pressed his lips together and returned no reply. It was plain that his mind was entirely made up!

I shall not linger on the details of the trial. It was swift and to the point. I stood up before a crowd of hostile eyes and told my simple narrative. It was too absurd to be given credence for an instant. I was considered not even a good liar. That a man I had never seen should have gone to the sheriff with an appeal for protection against me, and that he afterward should have attempted to murder me on the open highway, was too absurd.

As for the decision of the jury, they did not have to remain out for five minutes. Five minutes more saw me standing before the judge, condemned to twenty-five years of imprisonment in the State penitentiary.

I, a boy of eighteen—and twenty-five years!

I would be forty-three when I came out! At my age, forty-three seemed almost the end of life.

I shall not ask you to sit in my cell with me in the first wild hours of my anguish. I shall leap ahead to the evening of that day when the sheriff brought in to see me a gray-haired, lean-faced man with an eye wonderfully blue and bright.

I remembered him instantly. It was he who had chosen to back me against Harry Chase on the day of our second fight.

He said, cheerfully: "Youngster, you seem to have dropped into a bit of hard luck!"

I could not help breaking out: "I'm done for now. I've got life in prison, or practically that. I'm not saying it because I hope anyone will believe me, but now I want to say for the last time I'll ever say it, and to a stranger like you: That I swear to Heaven Niginski carried a gun and fired the first bullet, and that everything I've said about him has been the truth and the whole truth!"

"Why, the devil, lad," said the blue-eyed man, "I know that perfectly well!"

"What?" cried the sheriff, who had been just a little impressed by the solemnity of what I had said.

"I won't say what my reasons are," said the blue-eyed stranger. "You wouldn't believe them, sheriff, any more than you would believe this unlucky youngster. But I know that he told the truth."

"I'd like to see how you know!" exclaimed the sheriff.

"I'll give you one reason," said the other, with a snap of his fingers.

"Let me have it, then."

"Is this kid supposed, around your town, to be a fool?"

"No. He's had a name for a good deal of sense—since he went to live with Father McGuire."

"Very well. Would anyone but a fool have told the sort of a story he gave the judge and jury—unless it had been the truth? As a lie, can you imagine anything worse and weaker than the yarn he composed?"

The sheriff was a bit struck, and bit his lip in thought.

"All kids are complicated liars," said the stranger.

"Darned if it don't sound pretty reasonable," said the sheriff. "But there was too much evidence!"

"Oh, I know a good deal about evidence!" said the other airily. "Youngster," he added to me, "I've not stopped trying to do something for you. But I didn't know what shape you were in until the other day. I was busy at some work which I suppose your friend, the sheriff, would not have liked."

Here he gave a calm, smiling side glance to the sheriff. But the sheriff said nothing at all.

"I'd like to know," said I, "what reason you had for wanting to help me."

"Don't put it in the past tense," said he. "I saw you knock big Harry Chase kicking. I saw you stand up to that multiplied fiend incarnate—Andrew Chase. I'll never forget it. The rest of the dubs and blockheads in this town wouldn't forget it, if they had the wits of a child!"

I expected the sheriff to explode with rage; but there was something about the cool manner of this man which discouraged explosions very decidedly.

He went on: "My name is 'Tex' Cummins. Will you remember that?"

"I shall," said I.

"Before I go——"

"Before you go," said I, "tell me what could have been in the brain of that Niginski to attack me the way he did! Was he crazy?"

"Not a bit. He had taken good money for that job. The game was to incriminate you, of course, if Niginski was killed. But the real hope was that Niginski would dispose of you, instead of vice versa."

"Niginski did not even carry a gun!" cried the sheriff.

"Bah!" said Tex Cummins. "Look up his record and see if he was the kind to go without a gun even to a dance!"

"But no one would have done a rotten thing like that!" cried I, more bewildered than ever, as he offered this solution. "Who in the world would hire a man to kill me? Who have I done a real wrong to?"

He merely smiled at me. "Youngsters are always like that," said he. "They either think that everybody in the world is a crook—outside of themselves—or else they think that the world has no villains in it. Look here, Leon Porfilo, can you tell me that you have no real enemies around this town?"

"Only——" I stopped short and blushed. It seemed madness to attempt to connect the proud and wealthy family of Chase with such a brutal affair.

"Only what?" said Cummins. "I'm not the sheriff. I'm not the judge and the jury. But I'm the man who knows all about this. Let me hear you guess!"

"Harry Chase!" exclaimed I.

"Nonsense!" shouted the sheriff.

"Is it?" said Cummins coldly, and he looked our sheriff deliberately up and down. "I think that the time may come when Mendez will sweat, because, like a crowd of blind fools, you people have turned this honest youngster, here, into a criminal. But he's right.

"Harry Chase is well again and practicing with his guns. His whole family knew that. Do you think that they wanted him to go out and stand up to you once more? Do you think that Harry himself wanted to do that, if there was any way of avoiding it and keeping his honor intact?"

It was the true explosion of a bomb. The sheriff simply gripped at the bars and gaped at Tex Cummins. I could not say a word.

"Well," said Tex Cummins, "I'd like to shake hands with your prisoner, sheriff!"

He did not wait for a permission which the astonished sheriff did not have the voice to give, but he reached his hands through the bars to me and I, as I closed my fingers heartily over his, blinked violently. I had felt a sharp edge cutting into the palm of my hand. I had received, also, a small vial.

The rankest sort of an amateur detective could have told that I had received something from the hand of the stranger; but our good sheriff was at that moment the most green of all keepers of the law. He was still tasting the strange news which Tex Cummins had brought. I think that in the sheriff's mind, from that moment, there was an innate conviction that this blue-eyed, insolent man was right.

At least, the sheriff lingered after Cummins had left, and he said to me:

"I dunno, kid. All I wish is for the right man to get it in the neck. Dog-gone me if it's possible that the Chase bunch could be mixed up in dirty work like this."

"I've never accused them," I pointed out.

"Are you a fool, an innocent, or are you a smart crook?" roared the sheriff suddenly.

I said nothing, of course, and he strode away filled with emotion, leaving me alone in that nest of cells. For there was no other prisoner in the place.

I did not wait for night and darkness. In a trice I was examining that gift of Tex Cummins, and I found that I had in my hand the neatest of all small steel saws—a saw with an edge as brilliant, as keen, and as hard as though set with diamonds. The vial was full of the best oil.

I tried that saw dubiously—it was so tiny—on one of the stout bars of my cage. Behold! The keen edge sank into the strong steel of the bars with an exquisite ease!

As a matter of fact, that was not tool-proof steel—that cell of mine—or I should not have had such an easy time of it. But as it was, I was able to make the saw glide deep into the heart of the bar in a few moments. When it grew hot in my fingers and deep in the steel rut it had made, I used the oil, and once more it glided into the metal.

I had to make two cuttings, after which there would be room enough for me to press my body sidewise through the gap made by removing the one bar. I started the two cuttings, therefore, and cut each bar almost through. Then I sat down to wait.

When supper was brought in to me—rice and syrup and tea with a big lump of stale bread—I chatted good-naturedly to the jailer to keep his attention from the bars. And I fell to work on my food.

I finished and gave him back the tray. In another ten minutes the jail was closed, the great locks turned, and the lights were off. That jailer had other business on hand for the evening, and he was anxious to be away.

I did not wait for the town to grow quiet with the night. I should have stifled, I am sure, if I had had to keep inactive another moment. Instead, I fell to work on my cutting, and in a few moments the bar was sawed through and placed with a joyous care upon the floor.

That was a scant third of my labor done. I had to run down the hall to the big window which filled one end of it. I had to cut through two of the bars which covered its face. I worked with a furious energy, thrilled with terrible pangs of fear when the saw squeaked; with blisters growing on the tips of my fingers and with my wrists aching from the incessant play back and forth.

But those two bars were divided, each in two places, and lifted gently to the floor. My way was clear.

I cast one savage glance over my shoulder as I heard, I thought, a sound at the front of the jail.

Then I was instantly through the aperture which I had made through the window. I slipped to the ground outside, and it seemed to me that the taste of the free air which I breathed was the most dainty food, the most exquisite perfume which I had ever enjoyed. Then, around the corner of the jail, walked a man with a light, long stride. He came straight on, toward me. I was half of a mind to throw myself on him, but there was something about his jovial air and the manner in which he whistled lightly as he walked that made me hope that he might pass me without observing me.

He did pass!

But after he had made a single stride more, he paused sharply, and I heard him say: "There is a bay gelding on the far side of the plaza, tied in the shadow of the trees. No one will say you are a horse thief if you take him."

And he was gone! It was Tex Cummins again!

I gaped after him until he turned the farther corner of the jail. But here was no time to wonder at him. I was turning my back upon my old life. I was preparing to start north for the cloudy blue of the mountains and the safety they might give me. I was preparing to leave Mendez forever, I hoped, and I would leave behind me only one stinging regret—that the faith in my guilt was so strong in the heart of Father McGuire.

Yet, as the first chapter of my life ended, as I stood there an outlaw and an escaped convict, with the dread of the law to hang over me forever, I had much to be thankful for. No one could ever take from me those pleasant memories of the blessed years that I had spent with Father McGuire.

Chapter Eleven

"Mike" O'Rourke

When I went across the plaza from the jail I was glad of two things in this world, and no more: Tex Cummins and the night—Tex because he had made my escape possible, and the night because it shut me away from the view of the townsmen. I found at once the horse which he had named, but it seemed to me that the undoing of the knot required an age. Two men, half seen through the darkness, paused on the sidewalk and muttered to one another. I was sure that it was about me, and I was in a fever to be off. Yet I had the good sense to get into the saddle in a leisurely manner and start off into the saddle in a mild-mannered gallop.

I had to keep a stiff pull on the reins for that purpose, because the horse which my mysterious friend Cummins had provided was fairly rearing to go. But at least the two fellows on the sidewalk made no attempt to follow me. I considered that my first triumph.

But, no matter how eager I was to be out of the town—
for at any moment my escape might be noticed—I drew
the rein for an instant in front of the house of good Father
McGuire. When I thought of my three happy years with
him, I was on the verge of calling him out to me.

I recollected that it would not have been fair to him;
it might have put him in the light of one who failed in
his duty to the law by having cognizance of the escape
of a prisoner, and yet it made my heart ache to leave
the town without saying farewell to him. All that he
had done for me ran like wildfire through my mind.
I think, indeed, that the entire fifteen years of my life
before I came to him could not have weighed against
a single six months of my stay with the priest. I loved
him more than I had loved my father; and he loved me
as a son.

I loosed the rein and let the gelding have more of its
head. So we darted out of Mendez and onto the northern
road. I had not the slightest doubt of what my destination
should be. All my life I had looked toward the piled blue
mountains on the northern horizon as toward a prom-
ised land. Now I knew that they should be my land
indeed.

So I choked the gait of the gelding to a long, rolling
canter which ate up the miles with an effortless ease.
Three times I stopped my good nag and loosened the
cinches and walked a mile or so beside him to let him
take his breath and cool off, for the night was hot. Then
we struck briskly on again.

When the dawn came, I knew how much Tex Cummins
had done for me by selecting such a horse. There must
have been some of the bone and heart of a thoroughbred
in him, for in spite of the keen work of the night, his head

was still high, and his ears were pricking now and again.

It had been a mighty march, but now I had my reward, for we were already in the foothills, and the great dawn-blackened mountains went storming up through the gray of the sky above me. They had seemed gentle marvels of cool blue, in the distance—they were bleak monsters with ragged heads, viewed at close hand.

I kept straight ahead, however, in spite of the fatigue of my horse, until the rolling lands tossed me into the heart of the more rugged country. I chose for my halting place the flat shoulder of a mountain fenced about by a scattering of young firs and pines. In the central clearing there was ample good pasturage for my horse. As for myself, I was hungry enough, but I was far more weary. In a snug roll of blankets which the kindness of Tex Cummins had provided behind my saddle, I rolled up and in the thickest spot of shade which I could find, I was soon soundly asleep.

It was early morning! I suppose that the sun had not been above the eastern mountains more than an hour on its way when I first closed my eyes, and it was in just the opposite place when I opened them again. I had slept through a full twelve hours!

What I first felt was a stab of hunger. It was something over thirty hours since I had eaten, and at eighteen, with six feet and some odd inches of strong body maturing, and after a huge ride and after all the weary, lean hours of fasting during my jail days of trial and imprisonment, I was in the mood of a python which has a winter's fast behind it.

But I forgot food an instant later. Something stirred stealthily in the trees and brought flashing back upon my mind the realization that I was a fugitive from justice, condemned to a dreary long term of imprisonment by the due course of the law, and in as much vital danger as though I had really murdered that queer beast, Turk Niginski, and not downed him in the fairest of fair fights.

The realization of what I was, combined with that sound among the trees, brought me whirling to my feet with a gun in my hand. In three bounds, there was the cry of a girl, half squeal and half scream, in front of me, while she went scurrying out into the open.

I stopped at the edge of the trees and considered her, running with the sun sparkling in the red hair which the wind of her speed had blown out behind her. She was such a pretty sight that I almost forgot to be afraid of the danger which this glimpse she had had of me asleep might bring on my trail.

I called: "Well, kid, what's behind you?"

It stopped her as though I had tossed a rope over her head and borne back on it. She halted and turned around on me. I saw that I should not have called her "kid." She was a bit too old and too pretty for that. She seemed about fifteen or sixteen; but she was not tall for her age, and that was why I thought she was just a youngster when she ran away from me. Perhaps fifteen or sixteen may seem young enough to you, but you must remember that I was only eighteen myself.

"What do you mean by calling me a kid?" said she, still gasping a little.

But the shock of that first fright was leaving her every moment.

I sat down on a flat-topped stump. There was no one to see. There was only an old shack of a farmhouse down in the cup of the valley with a stick of white smoke stuck on top of it and broken squarely across by the wind after it rose a little way.

"I didn't think," said I, "that a grown-up woman like you would be running away every time a man said good morning to you."

"Humph!" said she, and put her hands on her hips with a very fine air. "Do you say good morning to most folks with a gun in your hand?"

"That was just for luck," said I, "to cheer things along a little."

"You're a nervy kind," said she, and she chuckled a little. She even walked back up the slope and stood in front of me so close that I could watch the green of her eyes. For lack of something else to do, she took the thick length of silken red hair over her shoulder and began to braid it; watching me all the time the way one man watches another man—with suspicion, you know, and a sort of hostile interest.

"Maybe you expected someone else," said she, and she gave me a crooked little smile that sank a dimple in one cheek.

"Maybe I did," said I, grinning at her.

"Maybe a gun would've been in order for him," said she.

"Maybe it would," said I.

But I didn't like this thread of conversation at all. She was trailing too close to the truth. While I thought it over I took another tuck in my belt. It was already drawn up fairly tight, and this reef bit pretty deep into my waistline. She nodded at me as though she understood.

"Hungry, eh?" said she.

"Yes," said I. "Excuse me!"

For just then I saw a pair of long ears flicked behind a stone. I glided out my Colt just in time to sink a bullet through the head of a big jack. It rolled ten feet down the hill before it lay still, with the echoes still barking back at us from the upper hills. I got the rabbit and brought it back. I cleaned it while she talked to me. It was breakfast, lunch, and dinner to me, and I worked fast.

"You might bring up a bit of a fire for me," said I, "if you need something to do."

"You *are* crusty," says she. But she chuckled again and built the fire in the center of the clearing. I had rabbit meat roasting in two snaps of your fingers. It was a sweet smell to me.

"What are you doing so far away from home?" said I.

"Riding herd," said she quick as a wink, and she waved to a score or two of cows browsing two miles away.

I saw that she was not going to talk any more than she felt was healthy.

"What's your name?" said I.

"Margaret O'Rourke," said she.

"What does that make for short?" said I.

"A man with a good education," says she, "can pronounce the whole thing."

"I was always too lazy to study," says I. "I hate making a speech. Suppose I call you 'Mike?'"

She blinked at me for a minute.

"Do you think I'm in disguise?" says she.

She was a sassy young thing, but there was never anything more feminine in the world, from the turn of her ankles to the tilt of her nose.

"You ran like a boy," said I. "I didn't know, Mike, but what you might be one."

"Well," said she, "you're cool! I think I'll step along."

But I knew by the way she gathered herself together and stood up, that she didn't intend to go.

As a matter of fact, I had never before talked to a girl as I was talking to her. I think that I had even been a bit backward with them, particularly after my years with Father McGuire took me away from the company of them so much. But when a man has his mind full of the danger of the law, and squints twice at every bush on the hillside to see if there isn't a shadow of a man behind it; and when the flash of every leaf in the forest may be a glint of a gun with an eye squinted at you behind it—one forgets a good deal of self-consciousness even at eighteen.

I merely grinned at Margaret O'Rourke again and said: "I'm sorry that you can't stay for the rabbit."

It was nearer the eating point every second. Now she wrinkled her nose to smell the fragrance of it.

"I might stay, after all," said she.

I began to whistle a tune and stirred the fire, while she turned the sharp stick on which the meat was spitted.

"I suppose you won't urge me," said she.

"A girl named Mike," said I, "is pretty apt to do what she pleases. I've invited you once!"

She kicked at a pebble and sent it spinning off. It darted under the nose of my gray gelding as he was reaching for a tuft of bunch grass, and he tossed up his head and danced back, snorting. Then she stared down at me for a minute, but I could see her fighting against a smile.

"I've never met up with any one just like you," said she.

"Thanks," said I.

"I didn't say that I meant it that way," murmured Mike. "What might your name be?"

"Smithers," I told her. "Larry Smithers."

"Where do you hang out?"

The only town I knew of in the mountains was called Camden. I told her that I came from that direction.

"Been long on the trail?" said she.

"Just a spell," said I indefinitely, for I had not the slightest idea how many leagues Camden might be away.

"Which trail did you come?" said she. "The short one or the long one?"

"The short one," said I.

"That's why your horse looks so spent, I suppose," said she.

Of course that made me open my eyes at her.

She explained: "Because if you hit north through these mountains without knowing the trails, it'll be rougher and leaner work than you ever did before, I suppose."

"Mike," said I, "didn't you hear me say that I'm drifting south?"

"Drifting," said she, with a neat little emphasis, "is a pretty good word for it. You wouldn't call it really riding, I guess."

She jerked a thumb over her shoulder toward the gelding. Of course, the good horse was a bit tucked up from his work of the night before, and he was pretty heavily marked with the salt of the sweat that had worked out on him.

I was worried. Not so much by what she said as by her manner of saying it. Those green eyes had a twinkle in them as they watched me, and I knew that she was seeing my trouble and preparing to make the most of it.

"That horse is soft," said I.

"I could tell that," she answered, throwing the ball straight back to me so that my fingers stung. "I could tell that by the look of his shoulders—and his quarters, too."

I couldn't help taking a look at the gray. He was in the very pink of the best condition, and there was not the least doubt of it. It stood out all over his body. On the quarters of the shoulders the long, ropy muscles slid into tangles and out again every time he took a step.

But how could I expect a girl of fifteen or sixteen to know so much?

"How old are you, Mike?" said I.

"Sixteen, Joe," said she.

"I didn't say my name was Joe."

"I know it isn't Larry," said she.

"How do you know that?"

"By the black of your eyes," said she. "You never got that very far north of the Rio Grande."

"My family have always been travelers," said I.

"There's no clay between here and Camden," said she, and jerked her thumb at the gelding again.

It was braided and tangled in his fetlocks. I saw that she knew a very great deal too much. Half an hour after she left me, she might have the sheriff on my trail.

"I took a detour," said I.

I hoped that might serve to put her off, but she was back at me in a flash with: "Were they following you as close as all that?" said she.

I blinked at her again. Then I laughed and chucked all the cards on the table face up; not all at once, however. I was willing to let her know that I was in the wrong, but I didn't want her to guess in what way.

"As a matter of fact," said I, "I got into a fracas with the son of the sheriff down yonder." Here I waved to the south. "I took a punch at him. He hit his head on the floor as he went down, and it opened up the claret. The sheriff swore I'd used a club and started hunting for me. So I thought I might as well slide out for the tall timber. Sheriffs have a nasty way of soaking a fellow when they feel like it."

I said it very confidentially, and she nodded in a most friendly way.

"I suppose," murmured Mike, "that you used the same sort of a punch that dropped the rabbit?"

In boxing parlance—and that comes naturally to me after three years with Father McGuire—it was as though she countered with a nice right just as I led with a straight left. She caught me flat-footed and put me back on my heels, pretty groggy. I could only stare at her for a moment.

She was too clever not to follow up her opening. She hit me again before I could put my hands up.

"I suppose you hit him from the hip, just the way you did the rabbit?" said she.

From the time I began to live in fear of my life from the gun of Harry Chase and started practicing every day with a Colt, I had worked at a quick draw, and I suppose that shot had seemed rather neat to Mike. At any rate, it was plain that I couldn't bamboozle her. I simply blurted out:

"Do all the girls up here grow this fast above the eyes?"

"I have two brothers," said Mike.

She said it in a way that was as much as though she had explained that they had put her through a pretty stiff course of sprouts.

"They've stayed up nights studying with you, I guess," said I.

"They've been a pretty liberal education," admitted Mike. "Did you kill him, or just wing the sheriff's son?"

She asked it as any other girl might have asked if I had killed or winged a wild goose.

"It wasn't the sheriff's son," said I.

"You've got me all tangled up," said she. "Which is the right story, after all?"

"The one you haven't heard," said I. "Do you want it?"

She knew by the straightness of my eye that I meant business this time, and she flushed with excitement. But then she set her teeth and shook her head, almost as though she were angry.

"Look here," said she, "of *course* I want to know. But you don't have to tell me. I'm not a sneaking quitter. Whether you're in the right or the wrong, I don't know. But I like—the way you roast rabbit!"

She gave me that twisted smile again with the dimple drilled right in the center of one cheek. I loved that smile this time, you can be sure.

"Whether you talk or keep still," said she, "I won't go blabbing. The sheriff doesn't have me on his payroll."

I reached her in one jump. I took hold of her two hands and looked her in the eye.

"Green eyes," said I, "you're a square shooter! I'd back you for a good scout against the best man that ever stepped!"

She was a little pleased, I think, but she only said: "You've dropped your rabbit in the dirt!"

It took a bit of the gimp out of me. But I went back and found that the meat had only dropped in a clean bunch of grass. I picked it up and sat down.

"All right," said I, "I'm going to tell you the whole yarn."

"Wait till you're outside of that rabbit," said she. "And then you can talk."

A starved dog doesn't wait to be asked twice when it sees a bone. I was picking the small bones of that rabbit about a minute later, and I only had to let the belt out one notch. That rabbit simply evaporated inside me.

"How is it?" said Mike, licking her lips. I had offered her a section of the meat two or three times, but she wouldn't take it.

"It's a good beginning," said I.

"I know," said Mike. "It simply fills up the holes and gets the ground all leveled out for a real meal."

"Darn!" said I. "Here I've wandered away without the makings."

A moment later she got a sack of Bull Durham and brown papers from somewhere and chucked them to me.

"D'you smoke?" said I, chucking about half that sack into a paper. I squinted at her. According to the sayings of Father McGuire, ladies don't smoke outside of big cities. Leastwise, they shouldn't.

"No," said Mike. "But I have two brothers."

I lay back and gave her a look from head to foot.

"I like you," said I.

Chapter Twelve

A Stockholder

It isn't hard to have to talk about oneself, when you're eighteen. As far as that goes, it's never so very difficult. But I took a slant at the sun, and by the hang of it in the sky, I knew that it was about time for Mike to trot back home. So I had to boil down my story into a nutshell.

"My name is Leon Porfilo," said I. "My mother was Irish. My father came within a split second of being all white, too, but the last fraction of him was Mexican Indian. That's where I get my black eyes and my dark skin. Some people have called me a greaser!"

I stopped here for a minute and looked at her.

"I admire them for that," said Mike. "They were brave men."

It was a neat way of making a compliment; it tickled me in just the right place, and I was a little red when I went on. I told her of my training with Father McGuire, and my three encounters with Harry Chase. And I told her what had led me to the mountains.

She sat and thought it over for a moment with her square chin resting on her brown fist.

"It was that rich man named Chase, I suppose," said she. "I suppose he bribed Niginski to get you into trouble so that Harry wouldn't break his neck falling off a cliff named Leon Porfilo."

It staggered me again. It was a conclusion that I myself had not had wits enough to reach. It was Tex Cummins who had given me the first hint of that idea. Here was a little kid in her teens who popped right onto the truth at the first jump. At least, I had a pretty good idea that it was close to the truth.

"You ought to be a weather prophet," I told her. "You could read the mind of a northeaster, if it has a mind."

"I've got two brothers," said this queer girl. "So now you're all set to blow north?"

"That's it. With the horse Tex Cummins gave me."

"Who is this here Tex Cummins?" said she, pointing a finger at me.

But by this time I was beginning to be afraid of her. She knew too much for me. She was so much smarter and quicker than I, that, beside her, I felt like a fat steer beside a cow pony.

"I don't know," I admitted.

"Is he an old friend?"

"I've only seen him a couple of times."

"Humph," said the girl, and began to prod at the gravel with a stick.

"It's about time for you to be drifting home, Mike," said I.

"Look here," said Mike, "how did Cummins get to know you?"

"He saw me fighting Harry Chase the second time, and he bet on me when the rest were backing Harry."

"Well," said Mike, "I don't like the sound of him."

I gasped at her: "Why, he's taken me out of jail, fixed me with a horse and blankets, and——"

"And turned you loose without a cent in your pockets. You haven't a penny!"

"Darn it!" said I. "How do you guess that?"

Instead of answering, she twisted away from me, and a minute later she turned around and tossed me a little rolled-up greenback. I unfurled it and read "twenty dollars." It was the prettiest little poem I had ever read in my life, but of course I held it out to her.

"I can't take charity," said I.

"Jiminy," said Mike, laughing at me, "you *are* silly. Why shouldn't you?"

"Why should I?" said I.

"Oh, I have two brothers," said she.

"That doesn't answer everything in the world."

"It nearly does," said she. "If you knew them, you'd understand."

"You pack around a bit of spare change for them when they're in a tight corner?" said I.

She paid no attention to me. Her eyes were shadowy with more thinking, and although I felt pretty small about it, I tucked that money into a trouser pocket and wished that God could show me how any angel could be finer than this girl.

"I'm wondering about this Chase family," said she. "How many are they?"

"Three," said I.

"You've licked one of them three times," said she. "What about the other two?"

"Harry is about enough for me," said I. "I've licked

him, but it's always been a tight squeeze. He's bigger than I am. His father is rich and seems a pretty straight shooter. Then he has an older brother called Andrew."

"Andrew Chase!" cried Mike.

I was not surprised that she had heard of him. Not *very* surprised. I knew that everyone in the desert stretches of the range was familiar with his reputation, and it would have been strange if the stories about him had not wandered a little way into the mountains.

"That's the one," said I.

"Poor Leon Porfilo" said she. "If Andrew Chase starts after you, I suppose that's the end? Now that the law is against you, I suppose he wouldn't mind a little hunting trip?"

It didn't stir up my pride. I knew that I was a pretty good fighter, gun or knife or fist—but I knew that Andrew Chase was just a thousand times better. I simply shook my head.

"If he comes after me," I admitted, "I suppose that I'm done!"

"It's hard luck," said Mike. "Tell me one thing more."

"Blaze away."

"Are you going to go straight, Leon?" I had not thought particularly about that. To save my hide was my chief concern.

"I suppose that I am," said I. "I want to."

"*I* want you to," said she. "I want my part of you to go straight as a die! I've bought twenty dollars' worth of you, Leon!"

It was an odd way of looking at the affair, but then, everything about Mike was odd.

"All right," said I. "You have twenty dollars in me. I'll try to keep that much straight."

"Oh, Leon," said Mike, and she came a little closer to me, "keep all of yourself straight! The mountains have enough crooks scattered around through them already. I see them now and then. They fry in the sun all summer; and they freeze all winter. They ride a hundred miles to get drunk on moonshine whisky; and then when they're full of it, they ride another hundred miles to murder an old friend. They start out just sort of naturally sliding down-hill. They mean to be honest, at first, but once they're outside of the law—what can they do?"

"I don't know, Mike," said I. "What *can* they do?"

"Then if they can't do any better," said Mike, tucking her chin up into the air, "why don't they put a bullet through their own heads rather than to come to live like sneaking, stealing rats? Oh, I hate a man that would live that way! I hate a man. I'd hate you, Leon Porfilo—even if you *do* have such a funny way of telling lies!"

She ended on a smile, but there was so much seriousness in her that I found myself blinking and winking at her. You have no idea how she had grown in the last few minutes. I began to feel as though she were actually my elder; she had gathered me up into the palm of her hand, you might say, and was giving me a lesson, shaking her finger at me.

To tell you the truth, it threw the matter before me in a new way. Since society had driven me out, it seemed to me that the only thing to do was to live just as I could. I knew that society had been wrong in turning me outdoors. Then let society take the consequences! But Mike put a new face on matters. I told her frankly that I would hate to have her despise me, and that I would make a hard try to go straight.

"If you're broke again, ride up that ravine across the

valley," said Mike, "until you come to an old house over the creek. If you were to stand outside in the dark and whistle like this——"

She whistled twice, made a pause, and whistled again. "I'd know that you were there, and I'd come out with another twenty dollars—if I had that much!"

How could I answer her? I could merely stare. Then she added with her strange little smile: "If I had *forty* dollars' worth of you, I might nearly control the stock. Don't you think so?"

"Why, Mike," said I, in a rather wobbly voice, "why, Mike, if I can go straight, I'll——"

She changed her own voice at once and made it very crisp and sharp. "You'd better saddle your horse," said she. "It's about time for you to run along!"

I knew she understood that I had been on the verge of growing sentimental. I bit my lip and did as she bade me, like a very dumb, downheaded, foolish boy.

When I had rubbed the saddle marks off the gray and brushed him and rubbed him all over with a hard twist of dry grass, I cinched the saddle on him and dug my knee into his ribs to make the rascal let the wind out of his lungs. Then I came back to her, leading the gelding.

"I'm going to blow north," said I. "But may I walk a way home with you, Mike?"

"You may not," said she. "I don't like the silly look in your eye!"

It angered me, and then I twitched my brains back into good working order and saw that she was quite right. I had been growing pretty foolishly soft about her, and she had a right to jerk me back to my better senses.

I shook hands with her. "I hope that you'll never hear that your twenty dollars has gone wrong," said I.

"I hope that I won't," said Mike, with her green eyes very serious.

I climbed into the saddle. "So long, Mike."

"So long, Leon. Wait a minute. How old are you?"

A little spirit came back to me. "I've forgotten that," said I, and so I rode off on the northern trail.

Chapter Thirteen

Seeking Shelter

I felt very triumphant because I had, in a way, had the pleasure of the last smile at the expense of Mike. But it was rather a flat pleasure. By the time I had topped the next ridge of the mountains, though there was still a warm glow in the mountain sky, the valley was beginning to take thick pools of shadow, and the lights winked on in the windows of the ranch house far below me. At the same time a cutting wind began to comb across the mountains.

Ah, that wind! There are sailors who will swear to you that a storm at sea is a wicked thing, but I have always felt that it is the reeling, staggering, unsure ship that makes a sea storm dreadful. In the mountains, it is another matter, and the wind itself is the devil turned loose. I had my first taste of a mountain storm that night.

I had to lean far forward in the saddle against the sheer poundage of the gale that shot across the ridge, while my poor horse, desert bred, tried to stop every now and then and bunch its back and drop its head between its forelegs—and great shudders of cold went through the chilled gelding. However, I had to bear it, and my horse had to bear it, too.

I have been in worse storms than that one during my life in the mountains. But considering that this was the first, and that I was on a desert horse, and in the dark of unknown trails, I think that the combination was terrible enough.

Pressed up against the sky, I felt all that any poor man can feel who has climbed into a chair of power greater than he can use. I felt naked—naked of my cold body, and naked of my colder soul.

When I saw a thin, yellow, winking light before me, I did not pause to reconnoiter. I headed straight for it! Had I known that behind that single ray of light waited for me a whole group of the bitterest enemies— a whole posse with a sheriff at the head of it—had there been a fifty-thousand-dollar reward upon my head, dead or alive—I should nevertheless have done as I did—ride straight to the barn behind the house and put up my horse in the first vacant stall, and then, carrying my saddle and bridle, proceed to the door of the house itself.

I battered at it. Before there was an answer from within, a great handful of wind, scooped from the black heart of the gorge behind me, struck me in the back and set the whole house staggering and chattering.

Somewhere from within there was a sound of crashing pottery, and then the windy bang of a closing door. I cast one glance behind me at the rough edges of the ravine, towering high above me. The cloud masses which had shut across the face of the heavens earlier in the night were scattered now. Through the gaping rifts bright shafts of starlight struck down and showed dizzy glimpses of the black sky itself which swam behind the flocking thunder clouds.

I waited for no more. Like a scared boy, with all my hundred and ninety pounds of athletic bone and muscle quivering, I wrenched the door open and jumped inside. It took the full strength of my arm to press the door shut behind me, and the blast which the momentary opening of the door loosed across the room raised a great flapping and a tearing of papers, and a violent rush of oaths.

Now, with my shoulders leaning back against the door, I shrugged the chill out of the small of my back and blinked at the unfamiliar brightness of the light from a big, round-burner lamp on the central table.

I did not see clearly. I only made out three men, but just what manner of men, I could not very well tell, for the wind had stung the tears into my eyes in a thick mist.

I was very conscious, however, that after the storm of oaths, there was a black moment of silence. Then a heavy voice said without cordiality: "Make yourself at home. There's a chair yonder by the stove."

I hung up my saddle and bridle, and went to the chair beside the stove. While the heat waves washed legs and head and throat and belly, and sent the cold shuddering out of me, a gruff voice asked:

"Chow?"

"Yep," said I, and stretched my arms closer around the stove.

At my answer, one of the men had lurched with a groan of involuntary protest out of his chair and strode into a kitchen from which he came back with a tin plate, which he cast clattering down on the table. He spooned a great heap of brown beans into it, a chunk of white fat of pork, and tossed down a liberal square of bread. Then he poured a tin cup of coffee—the greater part of a pint.

I did not wait for my invitation. It seemed as though the last relics of the rabbit had disappeared into my vitals a long age since. Wind and weather and the labor of the ride and the vital strain upon my courage and my attention through so many hours among the mountains, had made me a more famished man than ever. I marched across that plate with a huge iron spoon in less time than any heroic charge was ever sent home in history. The host, without a word, strode again into the kitchen and returned with an iron pot which, still without speech, he settled with a thump before me.

It was half filled with beans and pork. I ate like a wolf, or an Indian, until I was through. Then, with a great sigh, with the bottom of the kettle almost stripped of its provisions, I loosed my belt to the last notch and settled back in my chair. As I did so, I raised my head to the level of a small mirror set against the wall.

It showed me my own face, my broad mouth, my blunt nose, and that square, heavily timbered jaw which, as Father McGuire was wont to say, was designed by a special Providence for the careless receipt of all the buffets which life was likely to send my way. I saw that, and the gleaming black of my eyes, and the glossy black of my Indian hair, and the high cheek bones which are the sign of that outcross of blood which has marked me so deep, and the swarthy skin now flushed with rushing blood in the newly welcomed heat of the room.

I saw all of these things, and then I saw, in the outer corner of the mirror, the dim picture of a man standing with his feet spread wide apart, leaning against the opposite wall of the room. I saw thick cowhide boots on his legs, and heavy corduroy trousers, stained on the thighs with a crust of dirt and grease—perhaps from an untidy habit of wiping his hands there. I saw a burly body and a woolen shirt opened at the hairy throat. I saw a bull neck and a seamed, stern face decorated with a lean fighting jaw and a pair of all-seeing eyes.

He seemed to guess that I was watching and considering him. For now he said: "Well, Porfilo, have you had enough?"

The name went through my heart like a jag of lightning through a summer sky. I leaned heavily forward in the chair and then, swinging around, I saw a last detail of his costume which I had not marked before—the well-polished steel shield of a sheriff pinned on the breast of his shirt!

I flipped a hand back for my gun. But the sheriff did not make a move for his. Neither did either of the other two. They merely leaned forward in their chairs with their elbows on their knees and regarded me with a sort of sad concern and bewilderment.

It was the telegraph, of course, which had given them a description. No doubt the wires had been working as they sent out the word of me from Mendez, and, with my height and bulk and complexion, it was not difficult to spot me from the most casual description. They could practically wire my photograph over the entire range.

"I dunno," said the sheriff, "but I hope that you come in here to give yourself up, Porfilo?"

"You have me," said I. "Will you tell me your name?"

"Richard Lawton," said the sheriff.

"Well, sheriff, here's my gun," said I, and I handed over the revolver which Tex Cummins had provided in the saddle holster of the outfit with which he had equipped me.

The sheriff looked down to it like a man in a dream. He folded his hands behind his back.

"Well, boys?" said he. "What am I gonna do?"

"It may be a stall," said one.

I pushed the revolver back into its leather.

"It may be a stall," replied the sheriff in the same tone. "I dunno. I dunno what to guess. But he wasn't so tuckered out that he *had* to come in here!"

"It's up to you," said one of his companions.

"Damnation!" growled the sheriff.

I could not imagine what they were talking about, except that it was me. Why the cold steel of handcuffs was not already securing my wrists, I could not dream.

The sheriff began to pace the floor. He was a huge man. He was as massively built as Harry Chase himself. My hundred and ninety pounds felt fairly elfish in contrast with him.

Then he stopped with his back turned to all of us. "He didn't know me," said he. "I guess that's straight, eh?"

"I guess that's straight," answered the pair in the same tone, staring earnestly at me.

"He come in and hung up his saddle and his bridle. You seen that yourself!"

"I seen it!" they replied.

"Darn his boots!" groaned the sheriff. "Ain't this a devil of a hole for a man to be in?"

"The law is the law, by my way of looking at it," said one of Lawton's friends.

"Darn the law!" said the sheriff. "I'm thinkin' about something that's more important."

"What can that be?"

"My honor, you squarehead!"

He was working himself into a greater and greater passion. For my part, the talk was so much beyond me that I began to be a bit worried. It was like sitting in the presence of three serious madmen.

A clock began to strike rapidly and rang out eleven o'clock.

"Bedtime," said the sheriff. "And what about him?"

There was no answer. The two scratched their chins and looked at me and then at one another.

"Aw, the devil!" said Mr. Lawton. "I'm gonna do this the way I want to do it. The pair of you can talk all you want, and you can let everybody in the mountains hear about it!"

"Not a word from me," said one. "Only I'm considerable glad that I ain't in your boots. I'm downright sorry for you, Lawton!"

All this time, while he fought out some inward battle, the sheriff had kept his back to us and his face to the wall, and his big voice had been quivering and booming through the room. Now he turned sharply and beckoned to me. I followed him without a word through a door that opened into a little side room with a snug bunk built against the wall. There was a tick stuffed with straw on it, looking deliciously soft and comfortable.

"You got your own blankets," said the sheriff. "You can turn in!"

I waited, without saying a word. I waited for the irons which would surely be used to secure me for the night. The sheriff seemed to understand my perplexity, for, as he went out, he leaned a moment at the door.

"I'll put you on parole, kid," said he.

It made me jerk up my head like a horse that sights the home barn.

"Do you mean that?" said I.

"I mean it," said the somber man.

"Then I'll take you on it! You can have my word of honor, Lawton!"

"Thanks," murmured the sheriff, and he gave me a queer, uncomfortable little smile. "I suppose I'll see you in the morning, then?"

"You will."

The sheriff tilted back his head and laughter flooded his thick throat.

"All right, kid," said he. "I got to admit that you're a rare one!"

I sat down on the edge of the bunk after I had spread out my blankets, and I tried to puzzle the thing out. What the whole disturbance was about, I could not understand at all, except that it was clear that there was a weight upon the mind of the sheriff just as there was a weight upon the minds of the others.

Perhaps I should have remained awake to think the thing out, and then I might have seen through the mystery, but after my exposure, the warmth from the food and the meal I had eaten served to put me into a drowsy humor; my brain was working like the stiff cogs of an unoiled machine. I curled the blanket around me, and I was asleep in another moment.

When I wakened at last, the storm was no longer rumbling, but the wind was whistling a keen song around the edges of the house. The sun was shining through the little window, and the noise of tins was in the big room, and a stir of voices. The sheriff and his friends were wakening.

I tumbled out as quickly as I could, and when I stepped into the living room, the first man that saw me was one of Lawton's companions. He gave out a wild sort of yell, as though he had seen a ghost.

"Name of Heaven!" cried the man. "Hey, Lawton!"

"What's the matter?"

"Lawton, come here!"

The sheriff came into the doorway with his sleeves rolled up and a strip of raw bacon on the end of his fork, just as it had been when he prepared to drop it into the frying pan. He threw up both his hands. The strip of bacon fluttered away and flopped in the middle of the floor.

"It ain't him!" cried Lawton. "It's his ghost!"

"I thought of that—but there's his saddle!"

The sheriff strode up to me in a black passion. "You stayed over!" he snarled at me.

"Why not?" said I.

"Why, darn your heart," said he, "how long d'you think I want you here?"

It was an odd question.

"I suppose you don't have to feed the boys in jail out of your own pocket," I suggested stiffly.

"Jail? Jail, the devil," said the sheriff. "Who said anything about jail?"

A weird little hope went through me; it was too fantastic to be put into words, I felt.

"I understood——" I began.

"You understood nothin'!" he broke in. "Or else you wouldn't be here!"

"Lawton," said I, "it may sound foolish, but as a matter of fact, this sounds very much to me as though you wanted to make an end of keeping me in any place. It almost sounds as though you figured on turning me loose!"

"Does it look that way?" sneered Lawton. "Why, you got eyes, then, ain't you?"

His sarcasm, however, did not affect me. "Very well," said I. "I have done talking. You may say what you please."

He glowered again. His passion seemed to be rising every minute. "Look here, kid," said Lawton, "I don't

aim to be hard on kids like you. But, worse that that—
I can't be hard on you!"

"Sheriff," said I, "I don't follow this. Will you say it in words of one syllable?"

The sheriff raised his big voice to its top note—and he had a voice which would have swamped the bellow of a mad bull.

"You young jackass!" yelled he. "Ain't this my house? Can I jail a fool kid that walks in and eats my chuck?"

Chapter Fourteen

A Running Start

When I told that story to Tex Cummins, a little later, he said: "How did you feel?"

I simply blurted out: "I felt like the devil!"

That was the truth. The sharpest emotion that I felt was simply a great shame, that I should have put a man of that caliber into such a position that he had to violate the law in order to maintain his sense of chivalry. It fairly knocked the ground out from under me. There was something so clean and direct and sort of childish about that attitude of mind, that it reminded me of Mike O'Rourke.

"My Lord," said I to the sheriff, "what sort of men do these mountains breed?"

That took him back even more than what he said had taken me back. He stood there scratching his chin. Both of his friends had come in. I call them his friends. I might just as well have called them his trained man hunters, for that was what they were.

"Look at this fool kid," said the sheriff. "He took me at my word. I give him a parole and he *takes* it, and he lives up to it! Now what in the devil am I gonna do about it?

"Look here, kid," said he, "what do I make out of you? You murdered a gent called Turk Niginski. That's what you go to the pen for!"

"If I live to be a hundred," said I, "they'll never have a murder against me. That man tried to send a bullet through me. He hit my hat instead of my head. That was my luck. His luck was to get my slug fair and square. But when they picked him up to take him to town, they couldn't locate his gun; and when they looked at my gun, there were two empty chambers. Y'understand? I'd taken a flier at a rabbit and missed it. That was what beat me. They said that I'd shot the hole in my own hat."

"Well, boys?" said the sheriff to his companions.

They merely shrugged their shoulders.

"Speaking professional, I don't believe a word you've said," remarked the sheriff in his rough way. "You been found guilty, and them that are found guilty *are* guilty. What twelve men decide on is Bible for every sheriff in this here country. But speaking man to man, I got to say that I believe everything you've said and a lot more. I think you're innocent."

I cannot tell you how it thrilled me to hear him say it. A vast faith in human nature was brought back in a wave of joy upon my heart.

He went on: "I'm gonna turn you loose. I wish that it had been at night so's nobody could see you leave my house. But it's got to be by day. So, vamose."

I was happier still. I went up to the sheriff and held out my hand.

"Lawton," said I, "when I thank you, I mean to——"

"Shut up!" said he. "I don't want to shake hands with you. I'm gonna give you a running start—for a whole hour. Then I'm going to start on your trail and my two bunkies with me. We're going to get you, too! We've got horses that are fast and fresh, and we know this country— which you don't, I suppose. We're going to get you, kid, and we're going to send you back to Mendez on the way to the State prison, with a little extra added onto your term for breaking prison. I'm a sheriff. I've swore to uphold the law. I'm going to do it. I'll run you down if it takes my last hoss and my last man!"

There was no doubt that he meant business. It scared me; but it made me respect him, too.

"Very well," I answered him. "If you're coming after me, I've got to tell you one thing in exchange for the white way you've treated me. If I'm caught, I go up to the pen for enough years to wreck my life. I'm not going up!"

"You're going to beat all the officers of the law?" said the sheriff with a sneer. "You're going to outsmart us?"

I looked at him without any anger. I suppose that the little stretch of time since I left the house of Father McGuire to go to jail had aged me more than all my life before. I was beginning to understand—oh, not very much, but a few of the corners of the world.

"I don't think that I can," said I. "I don't think that I can outsmart you, and I don't think that I can beat you. But when you corner me, you won't take me alive."

He was serious enough, at that, and scowled at me. "You'll fight it out, then?" said he.

"They took me up on a crooked charge," said I. "I've got a right to be free and to fight to keep free!"

"Have you?" said the sheriff. "Look here, my son, twelve pretty honest men looked over your case and

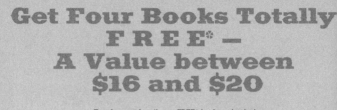

Get Four Books Totally F R E E* — A Value between $16 and $20

Tear here and mail your FREE* book card today!

PLEASE RUSH
MY FOUR FREE*
BOOKS TO ME
RIGHT AWAY!

LeisureWestern Book Club
P.O. Box 6613
Edison, NJ 08818-6613

figgered that you're guilty. Well, sir, because of that
you ain't got a right to fight back. What the twelve say
has to go for the law. Sometimes they make mistakes.
From what I've seen, they make more mistakes turning
guilty devils loose than they do sending up innocent men.
But when they do make a mistake, we got to stick by
it. It's hard on you, I admit. But it's better for the rest
of us."

"That's one way of looking at it," said I. "I don't see
it your way. I've got a gun, and I intend to use it. If you
corner me, I'll shoot five times to kill. I'll keep the sixth
shot for myself."

There was just a faint wrinkling of a smile at the corners of his mouth.

"When I was a kid, it was easy for me to talk hard,
too," said he.

It made me so proudly angry that I almost wished he
would start the fight on the spot. But I went out from the
house and sobered down when I found my horse. The gray
had stood up to the first and second stages of the ride very
well. But there was a good deal of fire missing from his
eye, and I knew that if I pushed him too hard on this day,
it would be the last real bit of work that I could get out
of him.

But in the meantime, I had exactly one hour to take
advantage of my head start!

I clapped a saddle on the gray, bridled him, and jogged
out into the valley. The country was rough, but just about
one per cent as terrible as it had looked to me in the
storm of the night before. As I looked at the crevices, the
tumbled stones as big as houses, the thickets and tangles
of trees, the twisting ravines, and the big mountains, I
decided that it would not be so hard to hide a whole
regiment here, let alone one man.

I timed myself by the watch. I rode straight for half an hour without trying to make any trail problems for the sheriff to solve. Then I intended to devote the rest of the hour to getting into a good hiding place.

I reached a stretch of hard rocks, then, and turned the gray onto them. What marks he made with his shoes would be hard reading on fresh-faced granite, I thought. At least, it was a trail which I should not have cared to try to decipher.

Still on those rocks, I turned into the mouth of a ravine and then worked my way to a natural covert among the rocks. There I tethered the gelding and sat down to wait. I waited a full hour. Then I found myself blinking my eyes and glaring in astonishment, for there came the sheriff riding, with his men behind him—three big men on three big horses, stepping lightly among the rocks, with the sheriff swung far down from his saddle to read the trail!

They had solved my little trail problem almost as swiftly as I had made it. I cursed them in my heart for men with eagle eyes. I looked around me for a way to get out, but there was none. I was backed up against the wall of the cliff, and to escape I had to ride out full in their view.

I threw myself on the back of the gelding and charged down at them desperately. They were in easy revolver distance—which means very point-blank range. They saw me the instant I shot into view, and three guns chimed like one. The poor gelding tossed its head and pitched to the ground.

I had only time to touch my feet from the stirrups, and then I opened fire. They had not remained in the saddle. They had taken to their heels after their very first discharge brought me down, and now they were running for cover, firing toward me at random as they ran.

It would be a very pleasant thing if I could tell you how I shuddered and shrank from the thing which lay before me. As a matter of fact, I didn't shudder or shrink at all. I simply said to myself: "There are three men trying to kill me, or capture me and give me what is worse than death. I'm going to nail them all or die trying!"

I thought that while I was rushing my horse out of my rocky covert. My first bullet was on the wing before the body of the brave gray was more than settled on the ground. It caught one of the sheriff's friends in the leg and dropped him on his face. My second shot was better aimed. It struck the big man who was just dropping into cover behind a rock, so that he threw out his arms and rolled out into full view of me. There he lay writhing.

I steadied my gun for a third shot.

I thank the Lord that I couldn't shoot, however; even with the cracking of the sheriff's revolver to urge me on. He was shooting very straight, but I was in such a position that he could not see me clearly. I tied a white handkerchief on the end of a stick and held it up—a bullet chopped that handkerchief in two and left only a ragged tuft of cloth wagging at the end of the stick.

Then I heard the sheriff yelling: "D'you give up? You yaller-bellied young swine!"

That was enough to make any man fight, and I shouted back at him: "They haven't the sort of men in these mountains that can make me give up. But both your men are down in plain sight of me. Do you want them murdered?"

There was a moment of silence, during which I suppose the sheriff maneuvered behind his rock until he could catch a glimpse of his two companions. What he saw made him yell back:

"You'll hang for this! But is there a truce?"

"Sure,' said I, "If I go clean free."

"Go free and be darned," said the sheriff, and then he was rash enough, or humane enough, to jump from behind his shelter and rush for his fallen friends.

I should have gone to help him care for them if I had been a true hero of romance. But I was not a true hero. I was simply a badly scared eighteen-year-old. I took the saddle and bridle and pack from my dead horse. Then I carried them over to the sheriff. He was paying no attention to the fellow who had been wounded in the thigh. But he was kneeling beside the other man, ripping his shirt off.

I did not offer to help. Neither did I feel any horror when I saw the blood. I looked into the drawn, pain-stricken face of that unlucky fellow and rolled a cigarette! It was callous, of course, but I had just come off with my own life by the grace of good fortune.

However, there was something about the look of him that told me he would not die.

"Do you want me to help?" I asked Lawton.

"You get the devil out of here," said the sheriff. "I've seen too much of you, already."

"I'm shy a horse," said I.

He jerked his head around and glared very angrily at me. "You've got the crust of a brass monkey," said Lawton. "Lemme hear what you want me to do about it?"

"Give me a horse in exchange for the one that you killed."

Lawton gave one more glance at the wounded man and then back at me.

"That's sweet!" snarled he. "I fix up a crook so's he can get away?"

"What else is there to do?" I asked him.

He twitched his big body around so that he could turn his back on me.

"I'll loan you any one of the three, if you'll ride back to town for a doctor," said he. "No," he added, as I started in, "don't take the black."

The black was his own horse. I was to know more about the qualities of that black later on. But in the meantime, I concentrated on the other pair. I have already said that they were strong horses, quite up to carrying my weight even in the mountains. I selected a pale chestnut mare with a rather Roman nose and an ugly look in her eye, but with four sound-looking legs and room enough where the front cinch ran to promise plenty of bottom. I dragged off the saddle and bridle which were on her and put on my own instead.

Then I mounted, and with her first step I knew that I had not changed my gray for a worse mount. The step of the mare was as light as drifting smoke. I have always thought that you can read a horse's enduring qualities and courage better by its walk than at any other gait. I like the rhythm of this nag's tread. I rode back to the sheriff.

"He won't die," I said.

But he did not return a word to me.

So I turned the head of the mare out of the ravine, and when I got into the valley I tried her gallop. It carried me along like a song until I came to a little huddle of houses at a crossroads—a wretched, cold-looking little village. I dared to ride straight into it. First I went on my own account into the store.

"Ain't that Jackson's hoss you got?" asked the fat old storekeeper.

"He loaned him to me to come in for some chuck," said I.

I bought some bacon and flour, some salt and sugar, some dried apples—and some ammunition for a Colt .45. Then I started out.

"Kind of young to be workin' for Lawton, ain't you?" said the storekeeper, coming to the door to watch me mount.

"Oh, I ain't so young," said I. "Besides, the sheriff will take a flier now and then."

"Has there been no track of that young Porfilo that's said to of hit for the mountains up this way?" he broke off sharply, and, staring as though he saw my face for the first time: "Why——" exclaimed the storekeeper, and then paused again.

I knew that he had recognized me, but I also knew that he was not the sort of a man to pull a gun even at as young a criminal as myself. I merely waved to him and asked him where the doctor lived. He told me that the doctor's house was at the eastern end of the street, set back behind a row of firs. I found it as he described it. It looked like a funeral, to be sure!

I put my mare at the fence, and she took it flying. Then I went winging up the path to the front door and fetched a kick at it that sent a crashing echo through the house. In a moment the door was whipped open and the doctor jumped out under the nose of my horse.

"Who's dying?" he asked.

"The sheriff and Jackson are in trouble. Jackson has been shot through the body," I told him, and then I described where I had left the pair of them. He wanted me to wait and ride to the spot with him, but I told him that he couldn't miss it—which was true—and that I would hurry back ahead of him. I hurried the mare over the fence again, put her down the street at a canter, and was beginning to gather headway when I heard a yelling behind me, and then I saw two fellers coming up the street like madmen, with the hat blown off the head of one and the brain blown out of the head of them both, I suppose.

It was red-eye, perhaps. Or perhaps they had simply heard the excited storekeeper speak of me and the calm manner in which I had dared to ride into their town. Such effrontery was an insult to every man in the village, of course. This pair decided that they would have to go after me. Perhaps neither of them would have had the courage, taken by himself. But a companion egged him on.

They had their guns out already, and as they came around the corner, reeling far off and shooting a cloud of dust out to the side, they opened fire. They worked from the backs of running horses. Their bullets went wide— yes, very wide!

I put my first bullet through the shoulder of the unlucky rascal who rode on the right. It must have been a frightfully painful wound. He twisted around in his saddle with a great scream of agony and pitched onto his face in the dust.

That was enough for his friend, too. He had a good excuse to stop his charge at me—he had to go back and take care of his unlucky bunkie. So he twitched his cow pony around and went back to the fellow who was kicking and cursing in the thick dust.

I went on up the valley.

I remember feeling that I was lucky to have only wounded them. But I did not feel it had been any great deliverance. Sooner or later, I decided, they would corner me, and my promise to the sheriff would have to be lived up to. In the meantime, one might as well be hunted for the killing of twenty men as of one!

Chapter Fifteen

In Hiding

By this time, I despaired of getting any headway toward a safe flight until I was better acquainted with that country. It was far too bewildering. I never could tell from what direction men might be riding toward me. I did not know which were blind trails and which were well-traveled ones. I did not know the difficulties of short cuts or the advantages of them. In fact, I knew nothing except that I was tossed down in a ragged ocean of mountains. In the meantime, I would have to get my bearings and establish some sort of a mental chart of my surroundings.

There was sure to be a frightful stir. Such a man as Lawton, impatient and bold and strong and sure of himself, would go almost mad with the reflection that a youngster such as I had stopped him, shot down two of his men, and then bearded the villagers in his town a scant mile or two away!

He would make enough trouble to occupy the attention of an army, to say nothing of the fuss that the men of the town might make, because I had had the impudence to go into their town in broad daylight.

The fact was that I had had no intention of doing a dare-devil thing. Even after the sheriff had recognized me, I did not feel that every other man would be able to do so. I had felt quite secure during that adventure. But now I saw that I would be known instantly wherever I appeared.

All of this was enough to make me decide to lie as low as possible for a time until, by quiet excursions here and there, I had mapped the country for myself. But where was I to hide?

I had never forgotten how my father had hidden a book from me when he did not wish me to read it. He simply put it on a shelf in plain sight—except that the back was to the wall. I combed the house from top to bottom and hunted in every closet, through every old trunk in the attic, through every nook of the cellar. But it was six months before I found that volume—by purest accident.

I decided that I should do the same thing with the sheriff. Wits I could not match against him. I felt that the coolest place for me would be on the very edge of the danger itself! So I went right back up the creek until I saw the peaked roof of his house to my left. Then I rode up a trail where the path came down to a ford, so that the prints of my horse would be lost in a tangle of other signs.

In a hundred yards I dipped to the right into a thick wooded place. When I came to the first clearing I decided that this would have to be my home. There was forage here for my mare. I had my blankets and food. There was very little chance that they would comb the country so close to the house of the sheriff!

The two dangers which I had to keep in mind were first, that the fire which was essential for cookery might be seen; second, that the mare might neigh if she heard another horse going down the trail. As for the mare, she was a sensitive, intelligent creature, and when she was startled by any sound in the woods, I could soothe her by speaking softly. She got so that she would come right up to me and nuzzle my hand like a dog.

As for the fire, I did my cooking at night because by day the smoke was sure to be seen. At night, I built my fire among a nest of rocks which screened the light very effectually, and I worked with a small, low flame, always. It used to take me two hours to do my cookery every other day. For ten whole days I remained in this spot.

In the afternoons I would venture up the face of the mountain which jumped at the sky right behind my covert. It looked over the rest of the lower mountains and the tangle of ravines and the little hollows and valleys which cut the face of the landscape. These I mapped in my mind as well as I could. Through the clear mountain air, I could look for limitless miles, and see far off the trails which twisted here and there.

When I had studied until my mind was full, I would steal back to the clearing and draw a map as accurately as I could remember each detail, even down to the trails. The next day, I carried my map with me and corrected it. Each day I studied more, until I began to have a deep familiarity with the items of that wide spread of mountains.

Only where peaks as lofty as my own went up from the general mass of roughness, there had to be blind spots in my knowledge. But I had a great mass of directions and localities and landmarks listed in due order.

On the tenth afternoon, when I came back through the mist and color of the sunset time, I smelled cigarette smoke from my clearing, and I knew that my hiding place had been discovered.

Of course I decided first to sneak away. But a second thought made me go on. I wanted to have a glance at the peculiar spy who, having found my rendezvous, had the folly to sit down and smoke at leisure in it! I wanted to see how many were in his party!

I came along with the care of a hunting snake and not much more noise, I think. Finally, when I reached the edge of the clearing, I saw only one man. He had his back to a tree; the side of his face was turned toward me; his hat was in his lap, and I saw the most welcome sight I could have wished for—the gray hair and the alert features of my benefactor—Tex Cummins!

"Tex!" said I, and stepped into the clearing.

He jumped up and shook hands with me.

"You're fixed up quite snug here," said he.

It was wonderfully good to hear a human voice after ten days of silence. The first thing I wanted to know was: How had he found me?

"Nothing mysterious about that," said Cummins. "When I heard that the sheriff had been working like a madman and had called out twenty of the best trail followers and sign readers in the mountains to help him, and when I found that he had worked for a whole week and hadn't come across a shadow or a trace of you, I decided that one of two things had happened.

"Either you and your horse had dropped off a trail into one of the rivers, or else you were tucked away and lying close under cover. I couldn't figure on the first thing. I could figure on the second. The more I thought of you and remembered that you are a pretty crafty youngster and not simply a gun puller, I decided that you had probably put yourself away right under the nose of the sheriff himself.

"I made his house the center, and I started cutting for signs from that spot. It has taken me two days. But here we are!"

It made me like him better than ever. In my first meetings with this odd man, there had been an air of reserve about him, a touch of mystery, something cryptic and "smart" in his speech. But now he was as simple and familiar as the most unpretentious man in the world. I could not help smiling upon him. At that moment, I had a real affection for him.

"This gives me a chance," said I, "to thank you for what you've done for me, Tex. I want to say——"

He waved my thanks into limbo. "Look here, kid," said he, "I got as much fun out of helping you as you got out of being helped. Maybe more! So the score is quit on that side of it."

"Let the gratitude go, then," said I. "I owe you quite a bit of hard cash."

"Very well," said he. "I don't mind having a few bits of money owing to me. It makes me feel that I have an anchor to windward."

He did not pause here, but went right on: "In the meantime, what are your schemes, youngster?"

I remembered Mike O'Rourke.

"I have only one scheme," said I. "I want to go straight."

Tex nodded at me. "I can tell you the one way to do it," said he.

"Fire away!" cried I, feeling that the mystery was about to be solved for me by his wits.

"Take your gun up and look it in the eye and pull the trigger," said my friend Tex Cummins. "Because the nearest place where you can go straight is heaven, my son!"

It seemed very foolish for a youngster of my age to contradict a man as clever and as filled with experience as Tex Cummins. I simply said, after a moment when the shock had passed off a bit: "Well, I may look around and find a way."

"Look around—sure," said Tex. "I wish you luck. I hope they don't fill you full of lead while you're looking. That's all. But tell me what you might have in your mind to do?"

"Why, I don't know," said I, feeling that my brain was spinning under the contact of this direct argument. "There ought to be a way."

"A man has to eat," said Tex, getting down to facts. "You admit that?"

"Of course."

"A man has to have company. You admit that?"

I had a hasty impulse to say that I thought a man might get on very well in some sort of a way, living by himself. But I felt that a lonely honesty would be rather dull with nothing but an occasional mountain goat for an audience to one's integrity.

"I admit that," said I at last.

"Well, how'll you get it?" asked Tex. "How'll you get food and companionship without being nabbed by the other honest men who are living straight, too?"

The very fact that he himself gave up the idea as an impractical one was about enough for me. Mike O'Rourke began to loom in my mind as a dear girl—but an excessively impractical one.

"It has me beat," said I.

"It has me beat, too," said Tex. "*I* tried to go straight. I tried it for years. I got jailed for something that I did in boyish ignorance, and I couldn't get my freedom although I broke away from jail because I was always recognized, as you will be.

"But with you, it's a different case. I had broken jail accused of fighting. You have broken jail accused of murder! There's a difference. I didn't pull a gun during the whole course of my wanderings. You've shot down three men and reduced a sheriff to the edge of a nervous breakdown. You have a build and a face that can be snapshot in a few words:

" 'Eighteen years old, looks like a Mexican prize fighter, six feet two, weighs a hundred and ninety.'

"That would hit you off. They *have* hit you off. They've plastered telegrams all over the mountains about you, and this little affair of Lawton and his trained man hunters has made everyone keen to get you; because the man that lands you now will make his reputation. They're going out in batches of three and four and trying their hands at amateur work. They've stacked up a twenty-five-hundred-dollar reward on your head!

"Now, my boy, I'm not a fool, and you know it. When I was a kid, I was a sharp youngster. But with everything in my favor, I couldn't beat the game.

"With everything against you, how can *you* expect to?"

He was so direct and crisp that there was no avoiding the conclusions that he reached. I felt that he was right. I *did* have to live, and when my money gave out, I either had to work for money or steal money, so far as I could see. How could I work honestly for it?

I told Tex that he was right, though it went against the grain to do it, and I was glad that Mike O'Rourke couldn't hear me say that. Tex nodded at me, and told me that I showed a bit of sense to agree with him.

"What I came up here for," said he, "is to tell you that I think I can show you how to make money fast and easy. It's risky business, but you're the sort of a fellow who enjoys a risk."

I told him that wasn't true. But he merely shrugged his shoulders.

"I've seen you fight with your fists," said he, "and I've heard how you fight with guns. How many kids at eighteen have killed their man and shot down four other men—each one a fighter?"

He went on quietly. He was all the more persuasive because his voice *was* so quiet.

"I saw it in you when I watched you fight Harry Chase. I saw that you were afraid of him, but I also saw that you were able to stand up and fight fast and hit hard in spite of your fear. In ten seconds, you were enjoying that fight. It was about the best fun you had ever had in your life. Isn't that true?"

I had to nod at Tex Cummins.

"Of course," said Tex, "it would be very pleasant if I could tell you that the only reason I have tried to help you is because I liked you and wanted you to get out of trouble. That *was* partly the reason. The other truth is that I thought I might be able to use you, one of these days. Now I think that the time has come!"

It was rather shocking, such frankness. But still I can't say that I didn't like him all the better for it, instead of hearing some sneaking, hypocritical excuses such as the way was well paved for.

He said: "I'm what you might call an employment manager of crooks, Leon. I don't do the actual work myself. I leave that to my men who are scattered here and there through the mountains and the desert. My job is to plan big things. I find the bank that can be robbed and I find the watchman or the clerk that will take the bribe to start things going. I locate the express shipment of hard cash and find out what train it is coming on.

"I get a whole lot of details that makes a whole lot of things possible, and then I make a split in the profits. The commission I take is a big split. I get half. But out of my half comes all the hush money that has been scattered along the line. You understand? Sometimes it costs a lot. I've actually pulled through a fifty-thousand-dollar job and found at the completion of it that I had lost a few hundred dollars after my twenty-five thousand was paid to me.

"Still, it was profitable because it gave a couple of my men a handsome profit. Other times, I clear up thirty or forty per cent of my share as clear velvet. But I have to pay out big money all the time. I have to take trips through the mountains. I find some rancher on a small place who is barely making both ends meet. I size him up, and if he looks all right to me I say: 'Suppose that a fellow should come along some day or night and say: "Partner, I need a fresh horse—or I need a meal—or I need a little cash—or I need some ammunition and a gun"— what would you do if he were to say: "Tex Cummins sent me?"'

"As a rule, they simply stare at me. Then I reach into my wallet and take out something. It all depends upon what I think of the man and the strategic importance of his house. Sometimes I give him fifty dollars. Sometimes I give him twenty—and sometimes I give him a hundred. I have the mountains and the desert dotted with such houses, son."

I could not help breaking in to ask him if he really wished to tell me so much about his private affairs. But he only smiled at me. He said that he hoped that this would be only the beginning of long business relations between us; and, in short, he told me that he was sure that I would make a successful life out of my career beyond the law.

I give you his reasons exactly as he gave them to me. He told me that most criminals are of course unsuccessful, but that is because they are stupid and uneducated, as a rule, and because they often have vital moral weaknesses—they cannot resist liquor, drugs, and a thousand other vices.

Above all, they have not the sense to associate themselves with other men who are trustworthy in their crimes, and the result is that the police are able to do most of their detective work by simply talking to the associates of suspected criminals. He went on from this to tell me that because I had been forced into a career of crime rather than made a deliberate choice of it, I had a thousand times greater chance of winning out.

"When I offer this opening to you, I have gone into detail so that you will have nothing to reproach me with hereafter. If you don't like my proposition, or my share of the loot, or any other feature which you see in it, you may back out now. There will be no hard feelings on my part. Every man who works for me hears just what you are hearing, and those men rarely break with me, because they know that they have to depend on me in the first place for the locating of good 'plants,' and in the second place for the measures which make crime safe."

I tried to tell him that it was not the safety or danger of crime to which I objected so much as crime itself; but he silenced me completely enough by telling me that I could take or leave his proposal exactly as I chose. He would not force me. After all, what was there for me to do? I felt that there was only one avenue open to me unless I wished to surrender myself to the police.

So, in another five minutes, I was sitting in the dusk of the day listening to Tex Cummins as he outlined what my next steps were to be. He had selected the thing for me to do and the man with whom I was to do it. Before the dark was firmly settled over the mountains I was in the saddle. Into the empty saddle holster he thrust his own rifle. He gave me fifty dollars—"in case anything went wrong"— and he shook hands and wished me luck.

I started away for my first deliberate violation of the law.

Chapter Sixteen

The Signal

My way held south, and at last was to pass down the valley near the house of O'Rourke. But the trip which had required five hours through rough going and in the teeth of a storm—five hours of agony—needed only two, now that I understood the lay of the land and had a mountain horse beneath me.

I whistled the signal which we had agreed upon—two short blasts, a pause, and then a long trill. After that, I sat down cross-legged, with my back to a tree, and waited. For it was a warm night, with a south wind straggling up the ravine and touching me with a friendly hand. There is nothing so human as the touch of a soft wind in the dark of the night.

Presently I saw a silhouette between me and the house. It was only for an instant, crossing the outline of one of the bright windows, but I thought that it was about the size of Mike. I repeated the signal softly. In another moment, she was standing before me.

I said: "Sit down, Mike, and rest your feet; I'm tired, and I suppose you're tired, too."

There was a flattened stump top just beside me, just a few inches above the top of the ground. Mike sat down on that.

"I'm not tired out shooting up posses, though," said she.

"You've heard about that?" I asked, with rather a thrill of gratification.

But she only snorted, and remained silent for a time.

"That's the way you're going straight?" said she.

I tried to explain: "I rode till I was half dead with the cold that night, and I blundered into the first house where I saw a light——"

"Oh, I know," said she impatiently. "The whole range knows all about it. Jackson did the talking. I suppose that Lawton wouldn't have said a word. Some of the thick heads want to fire Lawton, now, because he didn't capture a criminal—a murderer—when he had the man in his house!"

She was so savage about it, that I was really afraid of her.

"He's a fine fellow," I admitted. "I hope that he doesn't come to any trouble, because he treated me like a white man."

She grunted again. I began to grow angry in turn.

"I've come to pay back your twenty dollars," said I. I held out a bill toward her. She merely lighted a match and examined it. Then she blew the match out.

"I don't take stolen money," said she.

It was enough to make any one excited. I, being just eighteen years old, was boiling in an instant. I sat bolt upright and glared at her.

"Who said that I stole it?" I cried to her.

"Well, did you work for it?"

"It was given to me," said I.

"I hadn't thought of that," said Mike. "I hadn't thought that you might beg for what you needed!"

"Confound it!" I shouted at her. "I didn't beg for it! It was given to me!"

"For nothing?" said she.

"An advance payment on—some—some work that I'm going to do."

I could not help a slight faltering of my voice as I said this, and she leaped at my weakness instantly.

"What sort of work?" snapped Mike.

"Well, work is work. And it's none of your business," said I.

"Crooked money is just as bad before you've worked for it as *after* you've worked for it," said Mike.

I had one hearty wish, and I told her so. "I wish you were a man," said I through my teeth.

"No you don't," said Mike with the most infernal assurance. "If I were a man, you'd be afraid of me."

This impertinence made me see red. I could only gasp, and she immediately followed up her remark by asserting: "You're afraid of me even when I'm only a girl!"

"Well," said I recovering a little, "I have brought back your twenty dollars to you, Miss O'Rourke. Now I'll be getting on."

I held out the money, but she paid no attention to it. I folded it up and threw it into her lap. She brushed it away, and the breeze turned it slowly over and over on the ground like a dead leaf.

"Take it or leave it," said I. "I've returned the money to you. It was good enough for me, and it's good enough for you. Good night!"

I stepped to the mare, and I drew up the cinches with a wicked force that made the poor animal stagger and grunt. Then I jumped back at Mike and stood ominously over her.

"What the devil is the matter with you!" I cried. "Why do you treat me like a dog?"

I expected a stinging return that would crumple me up. But instead, she replied in the gentlest voice you can imagine: "Leon Porfilo, you're so big, and so silly, and so funny, and so young—I could cry over you!"

"Good heavens," said I, drawing myself up higher than before, "I hope that the time hasn't come when a little sawed-off sixteen-year-old kid can begin pitying me."

I saw her start in the darkness. "Am I sawed-off?" gasped she.

"The smallest I ever saw for your age," said I, rejoicing wickedly that I had found her weak spot.

"That's not true," said she, in a voice that trembled with emotion.

"Seventeen," said I, "and not even five feet tall!"

"Leon Porfilo, you're telling a lie and you know it! I'm one inch more than five feet, and I'm only sixteen!"

"Five feet tall with high heels——"

"I never wore high heels in my life!"

"A sawed-off little runt," said I, "taking on airs! Talking big!"

She jumped up in front of me. Then—I suppose because my bigness so near to her *did* make her seem small, she stepped back from me.

"I'm growing every day," said Mike. "What's more, do you think that I ever want to grow up to be a great hulking lummox like you?"

I felt that I had gained the upper hand, and so unexpectedly, so delightfully, by such small means, that I was able to laugh, loudly and long.

All at once she flung away from me and started running toward the house as I had seen her run once before—as swiftly, as gracefully as any boy. It sent a tingle of excitement up my back and into my throat. Three bounds of my long legs put me up with her, and then I scooped her off the ground.

She began to kick and struggle. It was perfectly useless. She struck at my face. I laughed louder than ever. I had formed such a huge respect for the youngster that it was astonishing to find her so small, so light.

Then an odd choking sound turned into a burst of noisy weeping, like the crying of a child. It was such a wild paroxysm that she lay helpless against my breast, moaning when she could take half a breath:

"If I could of—got to—the house—you'd never—never—have known! Let me go!"

I carried her back under the trees. I felt immensely pleased with myself and not at all inclined to pity her because she was crying. I felt, in fact, absurdly as though I had snapped my fingers under the beard of a lion and frightened the great beast into a corner of his cage! I sat down on the stump and held Mike on my knee.

It was really an astonishing thing to see the passion of her grief and anger. She cried with a stifled wailing—exactly like a child that is broken-hearted but afraid that it will be overheard. All the time she leaned against my shoulder and clung to me.

At last the sobbing began to stop. Eventually it ended altogether. What did she say, as she slipped away from me?

"I suppose I've made a perfect puddle on your shoulder, Leon?"

She had, in fact. The tears had soaked through my coat.

"How the devil was I to know that it would upset you like this?" I asked her rather mildly.

But she could still see through me. "You're mightily pleased with yourself because you've made me cry, Leon Porfilo!"

I declared that I was not, but it was perfectly useless to perjure myself about the matter. She merely sniffed and wiped away the last of her tears.

"Well," said she, in a voice of great relief, "it's a long time since I've made such a fool of myself as this. But it makes me feel a tremendous lot better. You've no idea!"

She sighed, and then she added: "Ever bump your crazy bone?"

"Yes," said I.

"Well, it's like that," said she. "When people mention my size, it's just like hitting your crazy bone. It makes me feel queer, and I cry like an idiot. But it's the last time you'll ever see a tear in my eye, Leon Porfilo—even if I'm not a great hippopotamus like you!"

I declared that I was grieved to the heart because I had hurt her feelings.

"You're not," said she. "You're tickled to death. You're disgusting the way you act, Leon Porfilo."

"As a matter of fact," said I, "I didn't suppose that you *had* any feelings, by the way you talked."

"How have I talked to you? I dare you to show me one thing!"

"As if I were a ruffian."

"Leon," said she, with a sigh, "I've been lying awake at night—swearing at myself because I cared enough about you to lie awake and worry. They've told us frightful things. They've told us that you must have been lost in trying to ford one of the rivers—because no green mountaineer could ever get away from a man like Lawton and his man hunters. I believed it, half. Now you come back to me with stolen money!"

"*Not* stolen," said I.

"Well," said she, "where did the man who gave it to you get it?"

"How should *I* know?" I said feebly.

I looked toward her miserably; and she looked toward me.

Chapter Seventeen

Steve Lucas

From Mike O'Rourke I traveled back to the main valley and rode on a good eight miles, until I had twisted out among the foothills beyond and saw in a hollow the scattered lights of a town. There was the end of my journey if I could find my man. However, the directions of my friend Tex Cummins seemed infallible.

I located on the outskirts of the town, staggeringly supported between two trees, an old shack with a rusty length of stovepipe cocked over its roof. It was utterly dark, but I did as Cummins directed me to do. I went to the door and rapped in a particular manner which he had prescribed.

I heard no approaching step, but presently a voice spoke close behind me:

"Well, where did you drop from?"

I turned and saw an armed man leaning against the trunk of a young aspen.

"A friend of mine thought that I could be put up here," said I.

"What's his name?"

"Tex Cummins," said I.

At that, he came closer to me and scratched a match. He held it dexterously in the cup of his hands, so that the light flickered across my hands, leaving him in darkness blacker than before.

"The devil," said he. "I didn't know that Tex knew anybody as young as this! What's your name?"

I was not angered. There was too much fear in me—of the work that lay ahead—to allow much room for personal pride.

"My name is Porfilo," said I. "What's yours?"

"You're Porfilo, are you? Well, that sounds better. You're the one that passed up Lawton and his boys the other day, eh?"

He shouldered past me and invited me to follow him into the house. There he lighted a lantern which he put on the floor and further screened with a heavy fold of newspaper. Not a great deal of light escaped, and what light there was filtered vaguely toward the ceiling. I had to guess at the face and the expression of my companion rather than see it clearly. He sat down on a broken box in the doorway, and most of the time his eyes were working restlessly down the slope toward the heart of the town; or sometimes he would rise abruptly and step to the back of the shack for a searching glance among the trees on that side of the shack. A caged tiger could not have been more alert.

"You dropped a pair of Lawton's pets, I hear," said this man.

"That was all that saved me," said I.

"From what?" said he.

"From Lawton. Lawton couldn't keep after me while I had two of his men helpless—able to bump them off at any time."

"Do you think that Lawton could have got you—when there was just the two of you left?" asked the stranger.

"The chances would have been five to one against me," I admitted. "He's a much better shot, and he's a lot smarter."

"By the heavens," said the other, "you're queer! Maybe it was just luck that you dropped the other pair? Maybe it was just luck that you put a slug through the shoulder of Dan Tucker?"

Here he reached out his hand.

"I'm Steve Lucas," said he. "Maybe Tex didn't tell you my name?"

"No."

"I'm glad to know you. I'm glad that Tex has picked up a bird like you that'll be a help to all of us. The only trouble is, they've plastered descriptions of you everywhere, and it ain't so hard to recognize you by the description. You won't be able to show your face by day. You'll have to be living by night!"

There was not a great deal of doubt of that.

"However," I suggested, "I suppose most of the work is done at night?"

"Not at all!" said he. "All the preparing, mostly, is done by the day. Speaking personal, I wouldn't follow no line of work that kept me up the night all the time. I ain't a sleeper. It's hard for me to get my rest even in the night. I can't bat an eye in the day after sunup!"

It was not hard to believe him. He could not remain quiet for an instant, but was continually fidgeting from one side to the other and glancing first at me, then at the lantern, then swinging about to shoot a glance at the rear window, then whirling again to scan the slope which led down through the town. There was nothing peculiar about his appearance—only the occasional glint of a golden tooth as he talked.

"I think that I can stand the night work," said I, "because I can sleep anywhere."

"Can you? Can you?" sighed Steve Lucas. "Well, you're lucky. They've slapped a price on your head."

He had changed the subject with a jarring suddenness, but I answered:

"Twenty-five hundred."

"Three thousand," said Mr. Lucas. "Three thousand even. Old man Castro brought in the coin this evening and put it in the bank to add to the reward. Three thousand dollars if they can nab you, Porfilo. Dead or alive! All that a gent has to do is to come up and sink a slug through the small of your back. That's the end.

"He drags you to town and gets the reward. Three thousand ain't so bad—considering that all a gent would invest would be the price of a lead slug! Even Wall Street couldn't beat that game for profit!"

"Thanks!" said I. "That makes me pretty comfortable."

"Aw, the devil," said he. "They got worse than that stuck on me. Six thousand iron men—six thousand juicy berries is all the luck bird collects that sinks me! Six thousand spondulics to the sucker that plants a bit of poison in my soup!"

"What did you do?" I asked.

"They hung the Walton job on me. After I bumped off Rickets, they gave me a rise and put up a twenty-five-hundred-dollar reward for me. But then I went along for a long time with just that reward on me and nothing more. Folks had sort of forgot about me. Then 'Whitey' Nichols the cur, he talked when they caught him. He laid the whole of the killing of Walton onto me. They believed his yarn, and so that got them excited. Yes, sir, six thousand bones is all they value this baby at!"

He seemed quite pleased with this dangerous honor. I told him that if he liked it, I wished they would transfer the three thousand from me to him, too.

"Aw," said he, "cut out the kidding. You know as well as I do that you're tickled to death because you made a fool out of Sheriff Lawton. How many of us wouldn't take a chance of having our heads blowed off for the sake of a reward offered, if we could have the name of havin' made a fool out of Lawton?"

"I didn't make a fool out of him," I insisted.

He shrugged his shoulders. "Have it your own way! Have it your own way! I don't give a tinker's darn what you think!"

He remained silent for a time, smoking a cigarette in a jerky way and flashing uneasy side glances at me from time to time. I didn't like Mr. Lucas. There was nothing about him that I cared for.

"Well," said he at last, in a better tone, "when they stacked the six thousand on my head, they made me!"

"How?"

"That was what brought me to the notice of Tex. Maybe that was what brought *you* to his eye."

I shrank from that unsavory suggestion.

"Since I went with Tex I've been making big money, for the first time."

"I thought he got a pretty big cut," said I.

"Sure. He gets his fifty. Which is pretty high. But then, he keeps you busy. And when you're broke, Tex will always float you through the shallows. He's white about that! What do you come in for on this job, kid?"

"I don't know."

"You don't know!" cried Lucas.

His ordinary voice was a sort of snarling whisper from the side of his mouth, and even when he exclaimed in this fashion there was more breath than sound. A sort of gasp.

"I didn't talk terms with him," said I. "He'll treat me well enough."

"All I know," said Lucas, "is that I get fifty. He can fix you up to suit himself, I suppose."

I said nothing. I liked Mr. Lucas less and less with the passing of every moment.

He fell into a dream.

"Maybe we'll make quite a haul. They's been some big deposits lately, I guess. Otherwise Tex wouldn't be going after the bank right now."

"A bank?" said I.

"Didn't you even know that?"

"I know nothing. I'm to learn from you."

He chuckled. "I'll show you plenty," said he. Then he added: "I guess that he wanted to break you in easy. This ain't much more than a one-man job. You know what I think?"

"Well?"

"This here may be a twenty-thousand-dollar job, kid!"

His voice trembled a little as he said it. He was as keen for money as a fox is for the blood of the goose.

Presently he jumped up.

"Are you ready, kid?"

"I'm ready."

"Then we'll start along. By the way the lights are going out, it looks as though most of those birds are roosting."

The town was as quiet as we could have wished when we went down toward it. Like most small Western places, it was strung out long and narrow, grouped chiefly along the one main street. We rode around behind it and tethered our horses under the shadow of some cottonwoods near the bank of a creek.

Lucas said: "This is straight behind the bank. When we've got the stuff, we can beat it straight back here and then ride across the creek. It's fordable here. I've looked over the whole place. I've spent a week fixing up everything. We can ford here—ride down between those two willows, and straight across. There's a deep place on each side, so be sure to ride straight. Then when we get across, there's clear sailing to the Custer house up yonder in the hills. Do you know Custer?"

I said that I didn't. He told me that the only thing I would have to think about was to keep close to him.

"That might be a good idea," said I, "but Tex Cummins told me that as soon as the job was done I had better take half of the stuff and leave you and ride straight back for him."

He had started walking away from the horses. Now he stopped short and seemed about to speak, but he apparently changed his mind, and we went on together. Again a wave of dislike for Mr. Lucas swelled through me.

We went through the back yard of a house, and a big dog came sneaking out and growled at us. Lucas threw it something which it gobbled at once, and then began to gag and moan.

"What was that?" I whispered.

"I had that dog in mind," chuckled Lucas. "It'll never growl at anybody else!"

I knew that he had poisoned the poor beast.

We crossed that yard and came out behind a low-built, thick-walled building of stone. I knew that it must be the bank. Lucas went up to the back entrance and took a key from his pocket which he fitted into the lock.

"How the devil did you get the key?" I asked him.

"Cummins attends to little things like this," whispered Lucas.

The lock turned with a well-oiled click, and the door opened. Inside, there was a whisper and stir of paper like a whisper and stir of human beings waiting for us in the black of the dark. But Lucas stepped boldly on and flashed an electric torch along the floor.

So he guided me to the front of the building. He posted me at the big plate-glass window. The broad shade was drawn, but I could look out through a crevice and see the watchman pacing up and down.

I sneaked back to Lucas and found that he had opened the door to the safe room and was kneeling in front of the safe. I touched his shoulder, and he turned with a frightened gasp.

"There's a fellow walking up and down in front of the building," said I. "Make no noise or he'll be in at us!"

"The devil, kid," said Lucas. "The watchman is fixed, if that's what you mean!"

I went back to my place of lookout. Perhaps it was from the watchman, also, that the necessary keys had been secured. Altogether, this was reducing the dangers of robbery to the minimum, and I wondered how few hundreds had been needed to corrupt this man who paced up and down the walk in front.

Once he stopped short just in front of me. Then he tapped on the window, and I tapped back. He made a reassuring gesture and went off to resume his beat.

I cannot tell you what a wave of disgust and contempt for that man went through me. It was as though a watchdog should lick the hand of a stealthy murderer. My wave of disgust embraced Lucas, Tex Cummins, and myself.

Robbery, on the face of it, had always seemed to me such a frightfully dangerous matter that I had always rather admired the talented and courageous criminals. But now that I could observe at first hand the treachery and the sneaking meanness which underlay this crime and, I had no doubt, most others of the same sort, it fairly turned my stomach.

I had a savage desire to jump up and tell my companion, as he worked away on the safe, that I would have nothing more to do with this affair. But I controlled myself. I had committed myself too far to turn back at this point in the game.

I heard the stealthy motions of Lucas—then there was the scratch of a match and a sudden fizzing sound. Lucas was suddenly at my side.

"Flat on the floor, kid!" he said.

I had barely time to obey when we heard a thick, stifled sound of thunder. No, it was rather like the exhalation of a gigantic breath that shook the building, rattled the glass, and seemed to make the very earth tremble.

By the time I had risen to my feet, I could see Lucas by the light of his own torch yanking open the drawers of the interior of the safe—and outside, the street seemed to be sleeping as peaceful as before.

No, yonder a light winked on in a window. Yonder, too, was the sound of a slammed door. Had some one come out to listen? Or were they coming to investigate?

I slipped back to Lucas with this information. He did not hear me. He was throwing bundle after bundle of greenbacks into the yawning mouth of a sack.

He talked in a chattering voice like a man with chills. "It's big! Oh, kid, it's big! We're made! We're fixed for life, I tell you!"

Suddenly a hand began to beat on the front door of the bank. But Lucas was already prepared to leave, or nearly so. In another instant he had scooped up the last of the bundles and thrown it into his bulging sack. Then he sped back through the building as we had come.

We darted through the rear door and flew across the open toward our horses at the same time that a chorus of voices began to rise. Then a crash told us that the door to the bank had been beaten in.

We were already nearing the cottonwoods when half a dozen men, spilling around the back of the bank, sang out, "There they go!" and a gun cracked.

"Send a couple of slugs that way and scatter the fools!" called Lucas.

I whirled around obediently and fired three times into the air. I saw the pursuers scatter right and left. At the same time, I heard the crashing of a horse through shrubbery, and, turning my head, I saw two strange things. The first was that Mr. Lucas had rushed his horse out of sight through the undergrowth and trees toward the ford. The second was that my own chestnut mare was running loose with dangling reins!

One does not need a translator to tell one what has happened in the mind of another man at such a time as this. I saw that the haul had been of such huge proportions that the slender honor of Lucas had buckled under the weight of it. I was to get nothing but the jail for my small share of this adventure. Truly it had been, as he had said, a one-man job.

In the meantime, the scoundrel had slashed the reins of my mare and chased her away with a wave of his hand. Yonder she galloped! Behind came the men of the town with a rush. Aye, there was the roar of the hoofs of half a dozen galloping horses turning out of the street of the village and swinging toward me across the fields.

Nothing could have saved me, then, except the ten days which I had spent with that fine creature in the solitude of the clearing near the house of Lawton. For now, when she heard my voice, in spite of the uproar behind me, and in spite of the hornetlike singing of the bullets which a dozen guns were spitting at us, she wheeled around and literally swung back toward me with her beautiful long mane flying like smoke about her head.

I went into that saddle like a leaping wild cat. I struck somehow, and I stuck somehow. I had her switched around and flying for the creek before I was in the saddle. As I gained the saddle and jammed my feet into the stirrups, I saw that I had rushed upon more trouble.

Lucas had been right in one thing, at least. The creek was not fordable except at the spot between the two willows. It was not even approachable on either side of that spot. There the banks gave down easily on either side. But beyond that favored point, the banks were sheer walls. I had sent the mare forward, however, at such a sprinting gait that I could not check her now. Before me there was what seemed to me a frightful chasm of darkness. But I had no alternative. I drove the spurs in and raised her at that terrible chasm. She, like the great heart that she was, answered with a snort of effort and flung herself high and far.

As we hung in the mid-leap, I was sure that we would crash down in the middle of the glinting water far beneath us, but she had a wonderful carry in her effort. We shot on, and her forefeet struck the solid level beyond. Only her back quarters crushed suddenly in behind me as the crumbling edge of the bank gave way beneath the shock of her weight.

I threw myself out of the saddle and cast back my weight on the reins.

It was enough. With that anchoring weight tugging at her head, scrambling like a cat, she came to her feet. I had the ends of the broken reins in my hand in an instant, and off we went.

I did not flee straightway, because the pursuit was coming up on wings. Instead, I bore to the right, and effectually put a screen of shadowy trees between me and the rifles.

But this maneuver had given me an immense gain in time. The horsemen rushed first at the point where I had attempted to leap across—convinced, no doubt, that they would find my horse and me struggling in the waters.

When they found that they were wrong and that I had escaped by a miracle, they had to ride up to the ford, go down to the stream, walk their horses slowly among the stretch of rapid current and dangerous rocks, climb up the steep, slippery slope beyond, and all this before they could begin to ride at speed.

By that time, when I turned my head as I galloped and looked back, I saw a barely perceptible line of shadows break away from the low wall of trees over the creek. I had a pretty thorough conviction that no horse in the world could catch up with the chestnut once she had such a flying start.

I let her fly. Just as dim before me as the pursuit was behind, I saw the form of Lucas. The rascal was well mounted, but there was such a vast rage in me that I think I could have made my horse overtake a veritable eagle. Let no man tell me that the rider cannot transform his mount! The mare that night was inspired, and it was my transcending passion which lifted her to the heights.

Chapter Eighteen

Cornering the Rat

At last I ranged beside Lucas.

"All right, kid," said he. "When I saw the mare rear back and break the reins, I thought you were done for. There wasn't no good in me staying to get caught, too. So I came along."

I said nothing. I could not have spoken. Something in the ratlike furtiveness with which he jerked his head toward me made me see that he meditated something more than pleasant words.

I ran my thumb over the ends of the reins and made sure, by the glossy smoothness of the leather, that a knife had done the work. No break can possibly take place, of course, without leaving ragged edges.

I decided that it might not be a bad idea to give him a bit of warning.

I said: "I'm keeping an eye on you, Lucas. If you make a queer move, I'll shoot you through the head."

Mr. Lucas said not a word in reply. He merely busied himself with the work of getting his horse along as fast as possible. I reined the chestnut half a stride behind him— with my gun always ready—my nerves steady as iron, and my heart as cold as ice with fury.

That sprint across the level seemed to take the heart out of the pursuit. They had lost the sight of me, and when Lucas swung his horse to the right and galloped away to the north behind the screening hills, there was not one chance in a thousand that they would be able to pick up the trail.

Lucas seemed to realize it fully as well as I did. He did not maintain that killing pace for another mile, but checked his gelding to an easy jog trot.

Through all the hours that remained of that night we never stopped our journeying. Sometimes the horses walked. Sometimes they trotted. Now and again we let them roll forward in a canter.

In the meantime, I was thinking hard and fast. Back in my mind the hatred of Lucas was as fixed as ever. But I could suppress it enough to make other conclusions for myself.

A bank was no impersonal thing which could afford to give up a huge sum of cash. My own small fortune was in a bank. Suppose that a pair of rascals like Lucas and myself were to gut the vault of that bank in Mendez? Then if the bank failed—as it unquestionably would— where would my fortune be? But that was not all. I was a single man. I could bear the loss. What of the sick and the poor whose small savings were pooled in banks? What of the small ranchers by the score who doubtless depended on their loans from that same bank to carry them through the lean winter season?

We were drifting toward the region of Lawton's home,

and it was the nearness to that place that put the first idea into my head.

Now Lucas stopped, dismounted, and kindled a small fire.

"Sit down with me, kid," said he.

I slipped from the saddle. The good mare followed me and stood over me. On one side of the fire was Lucas. On the other was I, and between us the wind-harried flames leaped and were flattened, and tossed into struggling waves. Lucas dumped the contents of the sack upon the ground and counted the bills in each package one by one—each package secured by a wrapper of stiff brown paper.

The first two packets were one-dollar bills, and he cursed heavily as he counted them—a hundred dollars in each. Then came a wad of hundreds. Twenty-five hundred in that little batch! Some fifties were next—and then a hoarse cry from Lucas. He had struck a pack of thousand-dollar bills!

I listened to his chanting, drunken voice in a daze while the sum mounted to twenty thousand, to thirty.

"Fifty thousand dollars!" screamed Lucas. "And we ain't a third of the way through!"

No, we were hardly a quarter of the way through the pile. For when that count ended, Mr. Steve Lucas had cried out: "A hundred and eighty-nine thousand dollars! Oh, kid, we're made! Do we take this to Tex? What right has he got to it? Didn't we turn the trick? Didn't we? We split this half and half—and then we beat it! Am I right?"

He licked his thin lips, and then looked at me with a gaping grin.

Then the hate in me turned into words. I stood up and said: "I've thought it all over and decided where we're going with that coin. We're going to go to the house of Lawton. You understand? We're going to go there, and when we get there, I'm going to leave you and the coin in his hands!"

The eyes of Lucas widened as though he had seen a nightmare.

"D'you mean that?" he gasped.

"I mean it. You tried to double cross me a while back—outside the bank."

"You're off your nut. What would Cummins do? He'd never stop till he snagged you!"

"To the devil with Cummins and you and the rest of the slimy crooks!" I said to Lucas. "Get up and get on your horse. Or else grab your gun."

I wanted him to take his gun. There was nothing in the world that I wanted so much, for I had an inborn surety that I would kill this rat of a man if it came to a fight. He seemed to know it, too. He looked at me through another whitefaced moment. Then he stood up without a word and went to his gelding.

He had his left hand raised to the pommel of his saddle and his left foot in the stirrup—certainly a seemingly helpless situation—when he made his play. He flung himself back against the neck and shoulder of his horse and, snatching out his revolver as he whirled, he fired point-blank at me.

His own swinging weight beat him. The shock of his body against the gelding made the horse stagger a little, and that stagger threw the bullet wide. I had snapped out my own gun and fired a split part of a second after him, and Lucas dropped to the ground with a scream. There he lay writhing and twisting and sobbing and shrieking with agony.

I could hardly uncurl his body to see what damage my

bullet had done, and then I saw that he was frightfully wounded indeed! The slug had torn through both forearms. It had ripped through his right arm and then, flying up, it had smashed the wrist bones on his left hand against the steel pommel of his saddle.

While he lay there damning me, inviting my soul to the most furious deeps of hell, I made as good a bandage as I could and took a hard twist around each arm halfway between elbow and wrist. That turned his arms numb and stopped the bleeding. Then I took him in my arms and slung him into his saddle.

He sat there crying like a child with the unspeakable agony of those wounds. Then I took the reins of his horse, mounted my chestnut mare, and led him on.

We were half a mile from the house of the sheriff when he began to beg, and the rest of that ride was the most grueling experience in my life. I had to listen to that poor devil tell me that I was taking him to his death—that they would be sure to hang him—that I had ruined him already with my bullet, and that that was punishment enough.

Perhaps it was, but there was a cruel devil in my heart that night. The shock of seeing my mare running loose with dangling reins while the townsmen rushed at me across the field had not left me. It had not left me to this moment. I cannot honestly say that I have the slightest regard for the manner in which I treated the yegg.

Just before the house of Lawton he threw himself out of the saddle. He swore that he would lie there, but I merely paused to tie the horse to a tree. Then I threw him over my shoulder like a sack of wheat and walked on, carrying the bag of money in my other hand.

When I came to the front door of Lawton's house, I found it unlocked. I suppose it never had come into the brain of that brave and famous fighter that any criminal would dare to invade his very premises! I walked through the big living room and past the dining table and kicked open the door to his room. That noise and the groaning of my prisoner, which began again at that moment, brought the form of Lawton leaping out of his bed.

"It's Leon Porfilo," I called to him, "and I've brought you a prisoner."

I added: "I've got my gun ready, Lawton, and I've got you covered. If you'll promise to listen to me talk and let me go safe out of your house, we'll do business."

He answered me with a torrent of curses; then a bit of silence.

"I'll talk to you, the devil take your hide!" said Lawton. "Wait till I light that lamp."

He came out half dressed and lighted the lamp in the living room while I lowered my man into a chair. Lawton gave him one glance and then grinned like a bull terrier seeing trouble ahead.

"My old friend Lucas!" chuckled the sheriff. "Welcome home, son!"

Lucas, seeing the gallows before him, shrank into his chair and forgot the pain of his wounds.

First of all we washed and dressed his arms. Then Lawton locked him in the next room at my request. There was no danger of him attempting to escape. Those shattered arms and hands could not have so much as turned the knob of a door.

After that we sat down in the living room, and the sheriff regarded me with a calm wonder, if I can use such a word.

"I've seen queer ones, kid," said he, "but I'm darned if I ever seen the equal of you. What d'you mean by bringing in that rat? You and him joined company and then had a fight?"

"Are you glad to have him?" I asked.

"He's better'n a Christmas cake to me," grinned the sheriff. "What's in that sack?"

"A hundred and eighty-nine thousand dollars," said I.

I could not help smiling as the sheriff slumped into a chair and gaped at me.

"Well," said Lawton at last, "lemme see the inside of it."

I tossed the sack toward him. The bottom of it struck the floor and spilled about the feet of Lawton a tide of wealth. He fairly turned white at the thought of so much money.

"Where did you get it?" he gasped.

"From the Crockett National Bank," said I.

"I'm gonna go nutty in another minute," said the sheriff. "What does it mean, kid?"

"It means that I started to go wrong," said I, "and that I don't like the inside lining of that sort of a life. We got this loot, and we started away. Now here it is back again. That's clear, I guess?"

The sheriff pushed the money reverently back into the sack. "Kid," said he, "I got nothin' to say. Except—what are you?"

"A gent that's trying to go straight," said I. "Here's my first payment. Will it go?"

"I dunno," sighed the sheriff. "I've worked for twenty years grabbing crooks and talking to 'em after they was grabbed. But I never met none of them like you! Tell me what you want me to do, and tell me in words of one syllable, because I can't understand nothing special hard right now."

I did as he had asked. I told him that I had brought in Lucas because I had seen, during my ride, exactly what a bank robbery might mean to a thousand poor people.

Besides, I did not like the dirty ways in which crooked money was made. I told him, also, of the way in which Lucas had tried to double cross me in my time of greatest peril, and how I had managed to overtake him.

To all of this the sheriff listened with the greatest attention. The shock of surprise was diminishing, and he was able to follow all that I had to say with a shrewd attention.

"The main point that I see right now," said Lawton, as I finished, "is that you *are* square, kid! Besides, I ain't forgot that after you dropped my two pals the other day, you risked your neck to ride into town and send out the doctor. It saved the life of Jackson. There ain't any doubt that another ten minutes without a doctor's help would have been the end of him. But, son, even if I know you're square, what can be done about it?"

"I don't know," said I wretchedly.

"The point is," said he, "that no matter what you and I know, other folks don't see nothing except that you been condemned to prison for a murder, that you've broke jail, and that you've shot three men since—to say nothin' of this here rat, Lucas. We throw him in for velvet, you might say! What can be done for you?"

"I've got to have money if I'm going to live," said I.

"In a small way, I could give you a hand—when I ain't hunting you down!" He sighed and shook his head, very much perplexed.

"I have an idea of a manner in which I can make plenty of money from time to time," said I.

"Well," said he, "lemme hear you tell the way."

He defied me with his eyes to solve such an impossible situation.

"I can tell you simply enough. There is a great deal of

money in these mountains that is not in the pockets of honest men."

"You mean it's in the pockets of the crooks? Yes, I know that. I'd need a thousand deputies—and real men, every one of 'em—to keep these here mountains combed clean. A man can hide ten times in every quarter mile. Where did *you* hide, kid?"

"A quarter of a mile from your house," said I.

He threw up his hands with a groan of despair.

"I might of knowed that," moaned Sheriff Lawton. "Well, go and tell me how you can make an honest living while you're an outlawed man with a face that's as well known as if it was the map of the United States?"

"There's no good reason why I shouldn't hunt down a few of the crooks, from time to time," said I. "They have money. Here's my first job, which isn't so bad. There's six thousand dollars' reward for the capture of Lucas. That money comes to me."

"How are you gonna be able to claim it without steppin' yourself into a jail?"

"You'll claim it for me, and I'll claim it from you."

"Cool," said the sheriff. "Always cool. Enough brass to fit up a stamp mill. I'm gonna claim that reward and then pay it over to you?"

"You are," said I.

"Ah, Lord," sighed the sheriff, "I suppose that I shall. How come I'm always your handy tool, Porfilo?"

"Because we need one another," said I.

"It's the first rim of the day stickin' over the hills yonder," said my friend Lawton. "If you're seen sneakin' around my house, I'm a ruined man and you're a lost man. Get out of here. Come back in a week. Tap at my window, and I'll pass your money out of the window to you. But after that, kid, I'm after you on your trail again. You understand?"

I understood clearly enough, and I left the house at once. I gathered from the sheriff that during the next week he would allow me a truce. So I spent the next day and the next night resting in my old clearing near his house.

After that, I dropped across the mountains on the chestnut and reached a little crossroads town at the junction of two big ravines. I got hold of a newspaper.

According to the paper, there was no doubt about Lucas' guilt. Perhaps it was the effect of the wounds which he bore from that fatal snapshot which I took at him with my revolver. At any rate, a little grilling from the sheriff had brought out a full confession from the poor sinner. In that confession, he admitted a career of crime which sickened me to read, and which I cannot repeat without loathing.

I was rather astonished to see that Sheriff Lawton had put down the facts in black and white. He began with a peroration which was typical of him, though I suppose that the reporter or editor had altered the grammar quite a little to the better.

What he began with was a naked statement of how he had first met me, how he had turned me loose from his house on account of his feeling that the spirit of Western hospitality is a sacred thing, and how he had pursued and failed to capture me.

He went on to tell how I had gone to town and sent the doctor back to the wounded men at sufficient risk to bring a fight on my shoulders before I was clear of the village. Then he told how I had come to him and brought the person of Steve Lucas, whose confession to many black and startling crimes was added in another part of the paper.

After that he shocked me by repeating exactly what I had said to him—that I expected the six thousand dollars' reward; for which I was repaying to the right owners the fifth part of a million dollars which had been taken from the bank at Crockett. Furthermore, I expected the sheriff to claim that money and to receive it from him. Beyond all this, he intended to give me that money before he started on my trail again, and he ended with a frank appeal to any voter in the country to impeach his conduct and his intentions and to criticize him if it was felt that he deserved criticism.

As for the criticism, I felt that perhaps the newspaper editorial summed up the possibilities fairly well. That editor was a born Westerner, and he declared in unhesitating language that the duty of hospitality impinged upon the officer of the law as much as upon any other human being. The sheriff, declared the editor, had done no more than right, and in promising me the six thousand dollars, he had made at least a fair exchange for a hundred and eighty-nine thousand.

Chapter Nineteen

Two Enemies

I was at the sheriff's window at the appointed time, and in answer to my knock, the sheriff thrust out his head almost at once.

He seemed in the highest of good humor.

"Porfilo," said he, "this here thing has come off in fine shape. Folks feel so dog-gone good toward you that I'm afraid I'd be lynched if I got you by shooting. They seem to figger that you've been partly unlucky and partly young—but that you mean right. Maybe you got more friends out of this fracas than you'd ever imagine. I've heard from the bank at Crockett. That bank went bust, my son, as maybe you heard?"

I told him that I had not heard.

He began to laugh. I have never heard a man so pleased with himself as the sheriff was on this night.

"Oh, yes. I'll say that that bank was sort of mild-ly pleased with the world when it heard that you was returning all that money. I've had the president of the bank up here. All he could say was that he wanted to have a chance to meet you and shake hands with you. When I told him that I couldn't manage that, he said that he would send along a little messenger to talk to you in his place. Here's the messenger. Open it, kid, and read it aloud."

He handed me the letter and held up a lantern at the same time. I opened that letter and took out five one-thousand-dollar bills. The letter read:

MY DEAR MR. PORFILO: We have received, in a complete accounting, all of the money to the last penny that was stolen from the Crockett Bank. I have called a meeting of the directors, and it is their opinion that something should be done to reward the extraordinary conduct which has returned such a vast sum of money to our vault. The more extra-ordinary, I may say, because we realize that this money is sent in by a man whose life is already endangered by a criminal judgment against him, so that it might be taken for granted that he would have ventured any crime in addition to that which is charged against him.

We have felt that your action is inspired by a real feeling both for the bank and for the numbers of unlucky depositors who would have been bankrupted by this great loss.

Accordingly, we have decided to send you a small token of our regard in the form of the contents which are enclosed with this letter. We beg you to accept them, and assure you that we wish our finances were at the present moment in such a state that we could make a larger reward.

In conclusion, after conversation with Mr. Lawton, it is our opinion that you cannot really be guilty of all the charges which are brought against you, and we beg to express to you our sympathy in your unlucky condition and ask you to call upon us still further should a time of need come upon you.

With many good wishes to you, we remain,

Cordially yours,

SAMUEL J. CROCKETT,

For the Directors of the Crockett Bank.

I read this dignified epistle several times through before all the meaning of it was digested by my befogged brain. Then I handed back the money to the sheriff.

"Lawton," I said to him, "I helped to take that money out of their vault and I don't deserve a reward for giving it back to them. But with their permission I'd like to take one thousand of the money they've offered me.

"I want to pay Jackson five hundred dollars for his horse, which I'm still riding. I want the other five hundred to go to pay his doctor bills and pay him, too, for all the time that he's laid up."

Lawton took the money with a grunt. "This is all queer," said he. "I think I'm gonna wake up and find that I've been readin' a fairy story. Now, kid, will you lemme give you some good advice? While all the folks are bustin' themselves with good things to say about you, I suggest that you give yourself up. I'll lay a dollar to a doughnut that inside of a week the governor will come through with a pardon for you. He'd be a fool if he didn't. It would bring him in twenty thousand extra votes at the next election!"

It was a tempting offer, of course. But when I reflected that the sheriff *might* be wrong, and what the alternative was for me in case he *was* in error, I could only shudder and shake my head.

"I can't do it, Lawton," I told him.

He sighed with a great relief. "Thank heavens for that," said he. "Then I'm gonna still get my chance at you in the open."

"You're going to get your chance at me."

"I'll nail you, son!" said he through his teeth. "You've made a fool of me once. You'll never make a fool of me again!"

I went away from Lawton's house with a strange feeling about him and about the world in general. There was no doubt that I had been wrong in my first conclusion. The world was not filled with selfish villains. There was plenty of good feeling and kindness and mercy everywhere. But could I trust to the clemency of the cold mind of a judge or of a governor to stand between me and half a lifetime of prison? I decided that I could not. No doubt I was foolish, but I ask you to remember, again, that I was only eighteen.

I went back to my Roman-nosed chestnut mare and rode her away to the south and the east down a trail with which I was familiar now. It carried me over a ridge and into a broad, pleasant valley, and down that valley until I turned into a narrow ravine, filled with shadows so thick that the light of the stars hardly could enter.

There I gave my signal according to the old agreement, and presently, at that place, I saw the shadowy form run out from the house toward me.

It was Mike, of course.

"Leon Porfilo!" called she from the distance.

I answered her with a cautious halloo. Then she was up with me and wringing my hand in both of hers.

"You *are* going straight?" cried Mike.

"I am," said I. "You bought twenty dollars' worth of stock in me, and that twenty dollars sort of outweighs the rest of me. I want to be crooked, Mike, but your share in me won't let me go wrong."

How she laughed, with her head thrown back.

"No one in the world guessed it," said she. "But what a lot of talk you've made! What a lot of things you've done—and all fine, Leon, since I saw you last!"

"And made a great enemy," said I.

"Bah," said she. "What enemy matters to a man like you?"

"I had one already. Two are too much," said I.

"Who are they?" said she.

"One is Andrew Chase," said I.

"Of course I've heard about him," said Mike. "But what's he? He's only a man. Who's the other one?"

"Tex Cummins," said I.

At this, she shrank suddenly away from me, and she looked up at me with a gasp of horror.

"Oh, Leon," moaned Mike. "Do you mean that he's against you?"

"I do," said I. "Does that make such a difference to you?"

For she was backing away from me. "Such a difference," said Mike, "that the best I can hope for you is that I'll never see you again!"

She turned back toward the house of her father.

I stood petrified and tried to make it out, but it defied analysis. I could only know two things. The first was that I could never follow the life of a law-breaker again. The second was that my first act of resolute honesty had alienated Mr. Texas Cummins, and with him I realized that I had lost the girl I loved.

Yet, no matter what mysteriously strong influence he might have over her, I knew that the victory was mine and that it was far better, at all costs, to go straight.

Chapter Twenty

Andrew Starts Out

It was Father McGuire who started Andrew on his search for me. They met on the road, and it was Andrew Chase who stopped to speak to the priest.

"You have not been particularly cordial to me since there was that unlucky affair of poor Leon Porfilo," said Andrew.

I suppose that the priest jerked back his head, and his eyes fired, as they always did when any one who was dear to him was mentioned. I think that he loved me more than he loved any other thing in the world. Had he not poured out upon me years of teaching and patient labor?

"I have avoided you lately," admitted Father McGuire with that warlike frankness of his.

"But why?" said Andrew Chase.

Not that he valued Father McGuire, but he was so used to admiration that it was rather a shock to him to be talked to in this manner.

"Because," said Father McGuire, "I have thought over the matter from A to Z. At first I thought that Leon might be in the wrong. I knew that he was headstrong. I knew that he was found of violence. But in time I have come to see that it would have been impossible for him to murder Niginski in cold blood. He was falsely accused."

"I trust that you are right," said Andrew Chase.

"Niginski was set upon him by some other person. There could have been no other reason behind the fight."

"Isn't that an odd conclusion?" said the big man.

"Examine your own heart, young man," said Father McGuire.

He would have passed on, but Chase, with a thrust of his spurs, planted the great black squarely in his path.

"Now tell me what you mean by that," said he.

There was never a very thick crust over the fires that burned in the priest. Now he broke out:

"It was you, Andrew Chase, or some other person in your family, who bribed the ruffian, Niginski, to attack the boy!"

With that he went on up the street and left Chase behind him. I have all the details of this scene which meant so much to my life. I had them from Father McGuire himself when I saw him again on a sad day.

Now I can dare to step into the mind of Andrew Chase to a certain extent and tell you what went on there. When he went back to his home, he turned this matter over and over in his mind. Whether he were guilty or not of the crime which Father McGuire charged to him, he knew that if the priest felt so strongly about the matter, other less kindly men and less judicious men must be thinking the thing, also.

Such a condition of life was intolerable to him. He could not exist except in that atmosphere of unqualified admiration with which he had been surrounded from his infancy. Two things he chiefly prized. The one was praise; the other was fear. If he could not be praised, he would be feared. But the praise was that for which he chiefly hungered.

He had never been without it. He had never attended a school where he was not the first scholar. He had never competed in a game where he was not the leading athlete, and I have no doubt that he told himself this suspicion was intolerable. He must remove it. How could that be done?

Where I was concerned, the way was cleared before him. I was an outlawed man. There was a price on my head which had mounted to three thousand dollars a very few weeks after my escape from the Mendez jail; and in the two years which followed that price had been raised, gradually, until now he who captured me was assured of the very substantial sum of seven thousand dollars!

The reward could not tempt him, but it pointed out to him that he could do a brilliant thing. He could remove this growing scandal which was spreading through the range about him.

He could remove it by removing the man whom he was said to have wronged. When he had disposed of me, instead of taking the handsome reward which was offered for my apprehension, alive or dead, he could make a fine gesture and crown himself with new laurels by turning over the entire sum to some popular charity.

I know from several events that followed later that this was lurking in his mind.

But, perhaps more than all else, I am sure that the sheer adventure for its own sake was a great impelling factor in the mind of Andrew. He had lived a soft life too long. The thought of danger was an inviting thing to him, and he prepared at once to make his journey.

I have no doubt that, no matter what his other motives, he would not have undertaken that ride to the north, through the mountains, if his goal had been any common man. But, by this time, rumor and gossip had piled up quite a heap of talk around me and made me a figure of some size in the eye of the Western world. The man who conquered me was sure to gain a great reputation. Andrew Chase decided that the time had come for him to put a bullet through my head and clap my little fame into his pocket.

It was when I was making an excellent bargain, that I first heard the grim news that Andrew was on my trail.

My horse was still Jackson's chestnut mare, which I had taken in the first place, and paid for in the second, so that no charge of horse theft could be lodged against me. On Jackson's mare, I started for the barren highlands above the timber line, and spent a day of laborious moiling and toiling before I got to the high places, in which I felt fairly safe. For it was not the first time I had gone among the cliffs and the heads of the great ravine for a refuge. I knew that high country better than anyone except an unshaven naturalist who tramped those dreary regions to study birds and flowers and insects.

It was not the fear of the sheriff and the hunting posses which had driven me to the heights, but the efforts of no less a person than Tex Cummins himself to destroy me!

I was well up in the rocks, when a disaster of the first magnitude overtook me—the chestnut mare went lame! I could do nothing but find a sheltered place in a great nest of rocks on the flat shoulder of a windy height and wait for her leg to become sound again.

I waited for two days, and she was progressing toward recovery. But they were two such days as I hope never to pass through again. Every moment of them I expected the sound of horses, and then the sound of guns.

When I heard a human voice from the ridge above me on the morning of the third day, I felt sure that I had been cornered at last.

I looked up quickly from my shelter, and there I saw, on the edge of the cliff, five hundred feet above my head, a rider on a big mule outlined against the sky.

No matter who it was, I felt that I was safe for the moment, at least. The cliff was almost sheer, and from that distance rifle fire could not harm me behind my broken wall of rocks. Then a yell of amazement and alarm tore its way out of my throat, for the mule pitched headfirst over the edge of the height!

I could not help blinking my eyes shut. But when I looked out again, toward the base of the cliff, expecting to see a confused, shapeless heap of beast and man, I found that the base of the rocks was still clean. Far up above me was mule and man, and still pitching down through thinnest air—yet not falling!

No, as a great mountain sheep pitches from a ridge and bounces down a frightful wall of rock, striking its feet here and there on almost imperceptible ridges to check the impetus of its descent, so that weird mule dropped out of the sky above me and zigzagged to the table-land immediately before me.

I watched the face of the rider during the latter part of that wild descent. He was a Negro; but he was not showing the whites of his eyes. He had leaned himself far back in the saddle, of course, to keep from overbalancing his mount, but otherwise he showed no more concern than

I would have shown in taking my chestnut for a gallop across prairie land!

When they were safe below, however, trouble began. The mule—it was a big, mouse-colored animal close to sixteen hands in height—seemed to be in a sort of happy frenzy, and having swooped like a bird through the air, it seemed to disdain its rider. It began to dance and side jump with pricking ears, while the Negro clung to the saddle with both hands, yelling: "Hey, you, Roanoke, you fool mule! Hey, Roanoke! Ain't you got no sense? How'm I botherin' you now? Hey, Roanoke! Quit it— or—"

Here Roanoke performed a maneuver something like the snapping of a whip. The Negro shot from the saddle, turned a somersault in the air, and landed unharmed— by good luck—on his hands and feet. As for the mule, since it had shaken off its rider, it started for the nearest outcropping of bunch grass, with which the little plateau was dotted, and began to feed.

Its master stood up and licked his scratched hands. Then he burst into a torrent of cursing. Finally he took Roanoke by the reins and drew a gun.

"Roanoke," said he, "I've knowed you, boy and man, for five years, and I ain't seen nor heard tell no good about you. If they was ever a dog-gone man-killin', wuthless mule, it's you. Roanoke, you is coming to your last day!"

He raised the gun.

I stopped him with a shout which startled him, so that he jumped away and whirled around on me with the gun leveled. When he saw my face he uttered a wild yell and dropped the gun to the rocks.

"Oh, Mr. Porfilo!" cried he. "I ain't meanin' you no harm! For de Lawd's sake, don't shoot, sir!"

All this time he had his two long arms stretched high above his head, and he was fairly dancing with terror.

Roanoke was already back at his cropping of the bunch grass. As for me, I had not made so much as a motion toward my gun.

"I'm not going to harm you, friend," said I. "Have you ever heard of me doing an unprovoked murder?"

"I ain't heard no harm about you, Mr. Porfilo," said the Negro, and he quaked more than ever.

"Put your hands down and take up your gun," said I. "Will you tell me if Roanoke makes a habit of coming down cliffs like that one?"

When he saw that I really meant him no harm, he recovered his spirits a little, but he refused to touch his gun, and merely kicked it to a greater distance, as if he feared that while it was near him I might misunderstand some chance gesture of his hands. I offered him the "makings," and he accepted them with a grin. His spirits began to rise at once.

"This here is something that I didn't never expect," said he. "I never thought that old Pete Garvey would be sittin' on a cloud smokin' with Leon Porfilo. I never thought of that!"

Below us there was a thin mist blown on the wind, so that there was some semblance of reason for this metaphor.

"Why do you want to kill your mule, Garvey?" said I.

"Because," said he, "I never know whether I'm gonna be sittin' in the saddle or standin' on my head on a rock, the next minute, while I'm ridin' that fool Roanoke."

I looked at the mule again. Even its head was smaller and better formed than I had ever seen in another of its kind, and it had the strong, sinewy neck of a stallion, with the body and legs of a thoroughbred. I pointed out those qualities to Pete, and he grinned again.

"That mule is what you might call a mistake, Mr. Porfilo," said he. "I was workin' for Mr. Morris Carney, takin' care of some of his fine hosses, and one of the mares went roamin' too far afield, you might say. Well, sir, when the time come, Roanoke come out in the world, and he's got all the brains and the meanness of a blood hoss and a jackass rolled into one! He's mean because he knows too much, not because he's a fool!"

I smiled at this idea, and then I asked him if the mule often made such a cliff as this one which he had just descended as an ordinary trail.

"He seen a mountain goat dancin' in the air one day," said Peter Garvey, "and he didn't never rest till he tried the same thing. First time it happened, I was huntin' along the edge of a cliff, and this dog-gone son of an eagle, he jest dipped over the side. I give one look to the sky, because that was where I hoped I'd be goin' when that mule got through drivin' a hole in the rocks of the valley that was half a mile under us.

"But he didn't drive no hole; he just went bouncin' and slidin' and glidin' down like he was half on wings and half on rubber. We come down, and when I looked back behind me from below, I says to myself that the good Lord, he sure done hitched a rope onto Roanoke and me. But about the next day he done the same thing. Dog-gone me if the nerve strain ain't plumb wore out this nigger!"

"Does he ever make a misstep?" asked I.

"Misstep? He's got some sort of glue in his feet, Mr. Porfilo," said Pete. "They ain't no way for him to slip. Now he could turn right around and run up that cliff with me on his back and think nothin' of it. It ain't what he does goin' up or down that I mind—it's what he does after he gets to the flat. He gets so riled up and proud of himself playin' buzzard and eagle that when he gets a chance, he does a dance like an Indian and lands me mostly on my head!"

He rubbed that powerfully constructed dome with great sympathy, and I cut short his sorrow by interrupting him and offering him a perfectly manageable—but lame—mare for the mule as it stood.

By the way of Pete Garvey in approaching that mare, I knew that he understood horseflesh. She was not a real beauty. Her head was spoiled with a Roman nose, and at that time she was thin enough to show every rib, which is apt to spoil the looks of a veritable Eclipse. But Pete Garvey was not bothered by superficials. First he examined the lame leg and then looked at me with an irrepressible grin which told me that he very well understood that it was only a minor ailment which could be cured by another day's rest. Then he went over the rest of the chestnut inch by inch. Before he finished, his grin clove his face squarely in two.

"Mr. Porfilo," said he, "I been always a mighty good friend, unbeknownst to you, and I dunno but that I might take this here mare off your hands to please you—and give you my Roanoke mule for nothin'!"

"Pete, you scoundrel!" said I, "that's a five-hundred-dollar mare, and you know it. Did you ever see a mule that was worth that much?"

"Did you ever see a wall-climbin' mule?" said Pete.

He was very much at his ease now. His life had been spared, and money had been put into his pocket. No wonder, then, that his chest enlarged, but his very next speech made me glad that I had brought him to a talkative mood, for he said:

"You bein' up here ain't because Mr. Andrew Chase is callin' on you, Mr. Porfilo?"

I presume that I changed color, for I felt the eyes of the Negro fixed curiously upon me.

"Tell me what you know about Chase," said I.

He told me what he knew, which was brief enough. Andrew Chase had entered the mountains freely proclaiming upon all sides that he intended to hunt me down and meet me single-handed. I felt, with a gripping chill about the heart, that Andrew would accomplish his purpose. The mere thought of failure could not be connected with his name.

I left Pete Garvey with thanks for his tidings, and I mounted the mule after I had transferred saddle and bridle to it. Pete assured me that that mule knew far more than any human being he had ever met, and before another hour was out I was inclined to agree with the Negro. Roanoke knew exactly what slope he could climb and what slope was too steep for him. He knew what cliff he could descend like a bouncing mountain goat, and he knew what one did not supply a sufficient number of footholds to check the downward rush.

How my spirits soared! By the cut of Roanoke's body, I knew that he had speed over the flat enough to keep off the rush of any cow pony; but I knew, also, that no mule ever bred could face the rush of a thoroughbred sprinter such as some of the outlaws and the men of the law kept in the mountains. However, unless one intended to fly straight down one of the long valleys, there were not very many opportunities to use a horse over easy terrain, and when it came to mountain work, those who pursued me had better try to catch a mountain sheep!

All the rest of that day I was gayly employed remapping, in my mind, all the trails that I knew in the region round about. Many and many a dizzy short cut was marked out for future use.

Not until the dark came did the thought of Andrew Chase return gloomily upon me.

For Andrew, in the meantime, had advanced into the heart of my country, and that very afternoon he had his first historic interview with Mike O'Rourke. It was not odd that he should have known that she was probably aware of my whereabouts; it was only rare that he should have had enough self-assurance to think that she would be apt to betray to him anything that she knew about me.

For the whole reach of the mountains understood very well that Mike and I were friends. They had known it well for more than a year, when I betrayed my hand by making a foolish present to her.

She had lost a pet horse—a beautiful little pinto with the eyes and the legs of a deer. It had broken a leg in a hole in the ground and had been destroyed. I, full of her sorrow, swore to myself that I would find something to take her trouble away, and I had in mind the very horse. Old "Cam" Tucker, who had a small ranch near Buffalo Bend, in the river bottom, knew horses better than most men know themselves, and the prize of his whole outfit was a dainty little cream-colored mare, not a shade over fifteen hands high, but made like a watch for compact strength and beauty. When I saw her silver mane and tail shining in the sun, I had thought of Mike on her back; when I heard that the pinto was dead, I struck straight back for Buffalo Bend and got at night to the place of Cam Tucker.

I bought a beautiful little mare off him which I presented to Mike. I had not thought that he would talk, but he did, and the tale of my purchase spread like wildfire.

So it was not remarkable that Andrew should have heard of the affair, but how could he have had the effrontery to go to her for information?

There is another way of explaining it. He may have gone, not in the hope of getting immediate information, but simply to find out how true the report of her beauty might be. If he satisfied himself that she was worth a little trouble——

Ah, well, that thought came to me afterward, when the damage had been done!

Chapter Twenty-one

Appealing to Mike

How much I would have given to be near when handsome Andrew Chase stood over little Mike O'Rourke, bowing to her as if she were a great lady, while the black charger, Tennessee, tossed its head in the background!

Ah, what a horse was Tennessee, and what a man was Andrew! How they were intended by Providence to set off one another! I suppose that Mike had never seen such a horse. Certainly she had never seen such a man, for though the best young men of the range dropped in to pay their respects to her, they were fellows who could not help polishing themselves up before they went to call.

They made themselves as gaudy as Mexicans, almost, but when Mike looked up to Andrew she looked up to a gentleman, and there is something in a woman which responds to that mysterious quality in a man. Not that she is always won by courtesy and the other qualities which go with gentility, so subtle, most of them, that they lack a name; indeed, she may prefer some rough-and-ready fellow.

She may like a good-natured clown; but she will know the real gentleman when she sees him, unless her eyes are already blinded by love. Then a tinsel imitation may do for her.

However, when Mike saw him I know that she knew him. I suppose that, under all the dust of riding, and in spite of the sweat and the grime, he seemed cleaner to her, in a nameless way, than all the other men she had known.

He introduced himself in the following way: "I am Andrew Chase, an old acquaintance of Leon Porfilo. But I see that you have heard of me, Miss O'Rourke."

For she had stiffened like a dog that finds *bear* written most legibly in the bodiless wind.

"I've heard of you," said Mike coldly. "I've heard of you from—him!"

No doubt she said it in a tone that implied a great deal. But it took even more to shake the calm of Andrew Chase. He merely smiled at her.

"I suppose that he has given me a rather black name," said he.

"He's a queer fellow," said Mike, "as I suppose you know—if you've had much to do with him.

"I've always thought him very queer," said Andrew.

"And square!" said Mike.

"Oh, very," said Andrew lightly.

She grew so angry that her eyes were dim. "Do you know what he has told me about you?"

"I have an idea," said he.

"Your idea," answered Mike, "is that he's said you are an underhand sneak who hired that Niginski to try a gun at his head; a rich man's son who used your father's money to beat him and run him out of the county so that he wouldn't get your brother into trouble; a bully who used your age and your strength to knock him senseless, once, after he'd fairly beaten that same brother!"

Even Andrew could not quite keep his face under such an attack, but he said:

"I haven't guessed that he would say all of that. I didn't know that Porfilo had such—an educated and lively imagination!"

"Oh, let's be frank," said Mike; "the same way that Leon is frank. He could have said those things about you, but he didn't. He simply told me that you are the best-looking man he knows, and the man with the best mind, and the strongest and bravest man he knows, and the man he's most afraid of in the world!"

She had a way, of course, of knowing how to startle people, and there's no doubt that she startled Andrew Chase with this talk. He only blinked at her and rubbed his chin.

"I know that you're joking," said he very feebly.

"But I'm not," said she. "I'm telling you the very honest truth!"

To this he replied gravely: "Then I have to revise what I've thought of him. He's just what you say—an unusual man!"

"Will you tell me why you came to see me?" said she.

"Because I expect to spend a good deal of time in this part of the mountains."

"Trailing poor Leon!"

"Exactly!"

This was her own frankness sent back to her, and she squinted at the handsome face of Andrew to make out what might lie in his mind.

"You've picked an odd person to tell it to," said Mike, beginning to glow again.

"I suppose some might think so," said he. "But since I'm to be around this part of the mountains so long, I wondered if you and I might not be friends—in a way—not real friends, perhaps—but friendly enough to say 'How do you do?' when we——"

She held up a finger at him. "You expect Leon to come down here to see me, and then you'll be waiting! But I'll warn him, Mr. Andrew Chase!"

"If you warn him, will that keep him away?" said Andrew.

She drew in her breath and then checked the words that were about to come out. She saw tragedy very near, and it frightened her.

"I don't know what to say," said Mike.

"Why," he suggested, "just say that, no matter what a war there may be between Leon and myself, so long as I fight fairly, man to man, single-handed, against him, there is no real reason why I shouldn't sit on your front porch once in a while or help you water the garden."

From almost any other person such talk would have made her suspicious, I have no doubt. But one couldn't very well accuse such a man as Andrew Chase of making foolish proposals to a girl he had met only a minute before—and under such conditions! If Mike was shocked at first, she was interested afterward.

"Well," said she in her open way, "you rather beat me, Mr. Chase."

"I'm sorry for that," said he. "But perhaps you'll let me explain why I have to go after Leon Porfilo?"

"I will," said she, "of course!"

"There is a great deal of ugly talk afloat," said he. "Some of it is absurd. Such as the rumor that I bribed

Niginski to go after Porfilo. That rumor has so much body to it that even a clear-headed person like yourself has taken it to heart a little, I'm afraid. Although I hope to convince you that I'm not the sort of a person who hires others to do his fighting for him!"

I think no one could have looked squarely into his calm, courageous eyes, as Mike was doing at that moment, and then accuse him of being a sneak and traitor. She shrugged her shoulders.

"I'm beginning to feel that I don't know what to think," said Mike.

"That's something for me to build on," said Andrew. "In the meantime, those rumors have grown and grown, until I had to end them one way or another. The only way I can find is to come single-handed into the valley and try to find Mr. Porfilo. Then, to be blunt and brutal, I intend to fight it out with him, man to man. In the opinion of the world, the survivor will be right. No, I think after such a fight, no matter what they have said of me before, they will agree that I wouldn't have undertaken such a thing if I were a sneak or a coward."

This was a reasonably fair statement, one must admit. Mike was just the person to see the reasonableness of it.

"Every one knows," said she, "that I'm proud to be the friend of Leon Porfilo. How can you ask me to be friendly with you, too?"

"Oh, I don't ask that," said Andrew Chase. "I've simply come to introduce myself and ask you to look at me not as a beast, but as a man—guilty of a great many faults, I know, but not of murder. I've come to see you because I intend to haunt this section around your house for a long time to come. I am not going to hunt Leon Porfilo. I am going to let him come down here to hunt me!"

It must have chilled the big heart of Mike to hear such a calm statement of facts.

"Knowing that I'll warn him?" she said.

"Taking that for granted, of course."

"It seems a terrible thing!"

"But isn't it fair?"

"I can't help saying that it looks fair. A man has to fight when his honor is attacked as they've attacked yours, I know."

That was the mountain way of looking at the matter. I can't help thinking that it was the right way of looking at it, too. But, oh, what a tragedy it put in store for me!

"I can't very well ask you into the house for a cup of coffee," said Mike, puzzling over him. "I can't—and be true to poor Leon. Yet I'd like to!"

"I'm as greatly obliged to you," said Andrew. "But, you see, I'd hardly be comfortable there. It would be like taking charity from Leon himself. I couldn't do that, you know!"

How could he have put it more neatly? And with that matchless smile of his to crown it all!

He said good-bye and stepped back to the side of the big, black Tennessee, and the stallion pricked his ears and nibbled gently at the shoulder of his master. They always made a grand picture, standing side by side.

Then, suddenly, from Mike: "I *am* going to ask you in!"

"No, no!"

"You're hot and tired."

"We'd both be embarrassed."

"*I* wouldn't!"

"But people have a nasty way of talking——"

"What do I care about people? They've wagged their tongues almost out about me, already."

"Then it would have to be explained to Porfilo. I can't put that on you."

"Nothing I do has to be explained to anyone—now that I'm eighteen!" said she.

You observe, Mike was always a little lioness. He, wise fox, from the very first appealed to her love of something startling—appealed, above all, to her courage itself.

That afternoon he drank the coffee and ate a fat sandwich which she prepared!

Chapter Twenty-two

Hot Words

It was no rumor of the meeting between Mike and Andrew Chase that brought me down the valley, but, making a swing down the western canyon, from Buffalo Bend, I dropped in on Cam Tucker. Whenever I was in that vicinity I used to drop in on him, and he was usually glad to see me.

He had made a very fair profit on me in our one horse deal, and after that the noise went abroad so far about the outlaw who had spent twelve hundred dollars upon one of the Tucker horses, that other people became interested in his breeding. His prices soared. He was able to double them within a month. Naturally, he was very grateful to me.

So that queer, rigid, fearless little man used to prop himself against the back of his chair and tell me all the news that he thought would interest me. He told me on this day of the bank robbery at Timber Creek. It had been a bad affair. When all was nearly said and done, and the robbers about to ride away, a one-legged cow-puncher had looked out of the window of his room across the street—because his recently amputated leg gave him too much pain to let him sleep—and he opened fire upon the suspicious forms coming from the bank.

There were four of them, and that lucky cow-puncher, with his plunging fire from above out of the mouth of a repeating Winchester, dropped two of them and killed a third. Only one man remained, and he got away with a small quantity of loot. Seven or eight thousand dollars was all that the bank missed. The bank, out of gratitude, had given the one-legged cow-puncher a job as inside watchman in the bank for the rest of his days.

I asked what description they had of the man who had escaped, and I was told that the men who had ridden for some distance in hot pursuit of him, blazing away with their rifles all the time, had made out a rather short-bodied man with extraordinarily broad shoulders.

It meant a good deal to me. I called up the figure of Sam Moyer at once. It was true that he had not been seen in these parts for more than a year, but that made it all the more likely that he would come back and try another fling in his old camping grounds. Sam had fled north of Timber Creek, but I knew fairly clearly that he would eventually turn and ride south, for he was one of Tex Cummins' men, and the houses of the friends of Tex were scattered south from Timber Creek, which was almost the northernmost boundary of the district in which he operated.

I found his trail and followed it until it brought me, just at the first thickening of the dark, into the valley and opposite the ravine which held the house of O'Rourke. Of course I could not give over seeing her now that I was so close.

I headed across the valley at Roanoke's shambling trot. His natural gait was not the usual mustang canter which rocks one across the miles without effort, but his swinging trot was almost as fast as the average canter—faster than some—and he was as unwearying at that pace as a wolf.

So he slid me across the night and up the darker ravine beyond, until I came under the trees opposite the house. There I dismounted and whistled the usual signal, my throat so closed with a joyous expectation that I could hardly make a sound.

She came at once, out the side door, and then running through the darkness to me. But when she came near there was no joyous greeting. She simply caught at my hands and shook them with her fear for me.

"Leon, you have not come down to fight him?"

"To fight whom?"

"You have not heard?"

"Nothing."

"He is here! Andrew Chase is here!"

It made me throw a startled glance over my shoulder, but then I tried to reassure her with a confidence which I by no means felt. For I was perfectly well aware, then and at all times, that Andrew Chase was a better man than I. By nothing but luck could I beat him.

"He's been here every day, waiting and watching for you, Leon. You must not meet him!"

"How have you seen him?" I asked. "Has he shown himself as openly as that?"

"Oh, he's as brave as a lion," said Mike.

"Humph!" said I. "Have you been talking to him?"

"Will you believe," said Mike, with a little drawn breath of wonder, "that he came to me and told me everything, very frankly? There is no deceit in him. He's as open as the day, Leon!"

What could I do except marvel at her; and the first dread came over me. I knew the smooth tongue and the easy manner of Andrew Chase too well, and I knew that there was danger in it. But now she was rushing ahead with the story. She was telling me how he came and how he met her; she was telling me how tall and how handsome he had stood before her.

"As big and as tall as you are, Leon, but——"

She stopped hastily here and went on with something else, but I had sense enough to fill out the uncompleted sentence. As tall and as heavy as I, but not with the ugly face of a prize fighter, not with beetling brows and swarthy skin and cold black eyes, and big, heavy-boned jaw; not with monstrous feet and huge hands; not with the bone of a horse and something of the clumsiness of a steer. I could fill in all that sentence for myself, and fear grew greater in me every moment—not the fear of Andrew's gun!

She had finished the story of how he sat in her house drinking coffee; then I broke in on her. That fear, and that grief, made me rude.

"You've been doing a fool thing, Mike," said I.

"What's that?" snapped out Mike.

"I tell you, it's dangerous," said I.

"What is dangerous?" said Mike, very cool.

"Andrew Chase. Do you think that you know enough about men to handle him?"

I should not have said that. She was eighteen, and at eighteen she was a great deal wiser than I at twenty, I have no doubt.

"I don't understand you," said Mike, "unless you are suggesting that Andrew Chase is not a gentleman."

"I don't mean that," said I. "Not at all! At least, he can *talk* like a gentleman. But what has talk to do with the real thing? Politeness is only one part, I suppose."

"You seem to know all about it," said Mike, more cold than ever.

"Mike," said I, "I suppose that I'm not to talk frankly to you?"

She stamped. "I wish you could have heard what he had to say about you!" cried Mike. "He didn't speak one thing against you. He didn't try to slander you behind your back!"

"You mean that I'm slandering him? I can see how it is. He has you charmed already."

"Leon Porfilo, how do you dare say that?"

"Oh, I don't mean that he's turned your head. But the way a snake charms a bird!"

"I'm a silly little fool like a bird in a nest, I suppose?"

"Mike, will you listen to reason?"

"I'm listening—but I don't hear the reason. I've never heard you talk like this before!"

"I hope to Heaven that I never have to talk like this again!" I exclaimed. "But I tell you what I know—that Andrew Chase is no good!"

"I don't believe it!" she answered tartly.

"Can a man be really good after he's hired a crook to shoot—"

"Oh, that!" she exclaimed. "He told me all about it. He told me how that foolish story started."

"Is it a foolish story?"

"Then tell me what real proofs you have against him?"

"If I had real proofs, I'd have him in jail, if I wanted to. One doesn't get real proofs of such dirty work. He's too smart to let such proofs float around."

"You've only guessed bad things about him. Isn't that true? Then you come to me and slander him. Leon, it isn't manly!"

I was desperate. "It has to stop!" I shouted at her.

"What has to stop?"

"You must stop seeing him."

"I must?" said she, full of danger.

"Don't you understand that he'll begin to wind you around his little finger?"

"Bah!" said Mike. "I'm—I'm ashamed to stand here and let you talk like this!"

"Mike, I forbid you to see him, and that's flat!"

Looking back upon it, I think that I must have been half mad to speak to her in such a manner—to Mike, of all the women in the world. I was not long left in the dark.

"You forbid me?"

"I do!"

"What right have you over me, Leon Porfilo?"

It brought me back to my sense with a jerk. "No right, only——"

"You owe an apology to him—and to me!" said she.

"Mike, I shall apologize to you, if you want me to. But I don't make any bones about it. I love you, Mike. It makes me sick inside to think of you in the hands of that fix——"

"Leon," cried she, with a voice that fairly trembled with anger, "I don't want to hear any more. I've heard a lot too much already. Good-bye!"

I took one step after her and dropped my heavy hand on her shoulder. "Are you going to go like this, Mike?"

"Will you take your hand away?"

"Very well! I'll never bother you again, if you wish to be left to Andrew Chase and his grand ways!"

"You coward!" exclaimed Mike.

It was like a whip struck across my face, and as I recoiled from her, she ran on toward the house. I did not follow again. I felt that in five minutes I had blasted away the greatest happiness in my life, and that I could never repair the damage which had been done. I knew, no matter how she might have felt toward him before, that this scene with me was almost enough to throw her headlong into his arms.

I went back to Roanoke and rode him slowly through the trees. We climbed the ragged wall of the ravine, and I was preparing to camp for the night, when I saw a light blinking four or five miles to the south. I remembered, then, the shack which the Ricks brothers, Willie and Joe, had built on the edge of the highlands above the valley. I remembered, too, that I had heard they were friendly to Tex Cummins. What was more likely than that Sam Moyer, whose trail had led toward the valley the night before, might be lying up and resting at the Ricks house?

It was enough to start me. After my interview with Mike I wanted action and lots of it. I wanted blood, and with the smell of blood in my nostrils, I started for the Ricks house.

However, I made no attempt to reconnoiter. I simply left Roanoke nearby and strode to the door. The jumble of voices inside stopped instantly as I stirred the latch.

"Who's there?" asked the voice of Willie Ricks.

The blind devil which makes men kill and gets them killed was certainly on me. "Porfilo!" I shouted, and gave the door my shoulder.

"Porfilo!" rumbled several voices within.

For my career in the past two years, preying on the thieves themselves and making myself fat with the spoils which their cunning had gathered, had made me as dreaded among them as a man-eating·tiger is dreaded in a Hindu village.

That instant the light was blown out, and at the same time I struck the door with my shoulder.

It was a good, strong bolt, well secured in stout, new wood, but the demon in me had no regard for wood or iron this night. I ground that bolt through the wood as though it were secured in hollowed paper, and flung the door wide as a voice barked—pitched high with half-hysterical rage and fear:

"Keep back, Porfilo! Keep out, or I'll shoot!"

That was my wide-shouldered friend, Sam Moyer, I knew, and as the door darted open before me, a pistol blazed out of the pitchy blackness within.

Chapter Twenty-three

The Big Scrap

I had pitched forward on my belly as I tossed the door wide. The slug from the gun of Moyer combed the air breast high above me—a well-intentioned shot, but fired just a trick too late.

Someone was yelling—I think it was Joe Ricks:

"Lord, boys! Are you gonna do a murder? Will you put up your guns? Porfilo, are you drunk? No, darn you, take it, then!"

I saw a shadow to the left of me, and I leaped at it like a dog off my hands and feet and knees. I struck that body and it went down with a yell before me.

"Help!" screamed the voice beneath me.

I reached for his windpipe, found it, and crushed my hands deep. The shout went out in a bubbling cry.

"Don't shoot!" yelled another. "Don't shoot, Sam. He's got Joe down. Knives, Sam!"

I knew what that meant. I surged to my knees and

heaved up the senseless form of Joe with me. He was a
heavy man. I presume he weighed not ten pounds short of
two hundred, but there was enough strength of passion in
me to let me throw him straight into the face of a shadow
which was lunging at me—lunging with a pale glint of
steel in front.

A muffled cry—a crashing fall—and that danger was
blotted out as Joe and the other tumbled in an inextricably
jumbled mass in a corner of the cabin, with a force that
seemed to threaten to tear out the side of the cabin.

I whirled back from that ruinous fall with my left fist
swinging as I turned, for I knew that the third man would
be leaping at me from behind.

It was in the last nick of time. His knife flicked a bit
of skin and flesh from the rim of my right ear; then the
side of my arm struck him and flattened him against the
wall. Before he could straighten up, I let him have it
with a straight right that bit into his face, through the
flesh, against the bone, and flattened him against the wall.
He hung there for an instant as though glued. Then he
crumpled gently forward and slumped upon his face.

He was ended—whichever he was—and so was Joe.
There was only the second man to handle and when I
gripped him as he disentangled himself from Joe's body,
I knew that I had Sam Moyer, for his body was a writhing
mass of the hardest muscle.

The knife had been knocked from his hand, and now he
was reaching for his gun. I got his wrist in time, and with
a twist burned the flesh and rolled the sinews against the
bone. That hand was numb and useless.

He dashed his other fist, with a groan, against my jaw.
It was like the playful slap of a child to me. I struck
with deliberation, up and across, with a toss of my whole
weight. The knuckles lodged fairly under his chin and

snapped the head back as though a sledge had struck him on the forehead. He fell backward and rolled upon his face.

Then I lighted the lamp.

I paid no attention to the men, but sought for the loot at once. It was simply padded into an old pigskin wallet, blackened by usage and much time. I took out the money and deliberately counted it. Either he had gotten rid of part of it already, or else there had been an overstatement on the part of the bank.

There was only forty-eight hundred and a few odd dollars in that wallet. I picked up the cash, crammed it into my pocket, and backed out from the cabin. I had filled my hands with pleasant action for a few sweet instants, and now I was willing to retire. It was not the money that mattered, though my stock of cash was at that moment rather low—it was the delight of the battle which I left behind me. Even the scene with Mike, and all the gloomy consequences which it foreboded, was forgotten for the time.

That sense of exaltation lasted long enough for me to find a new camping ground not four hundred yards from the cabin itself, on a grassy knoll with a sound of running water at the side of the open space. There, facing the east so that the first light would most surely rouse me, I stretched out within hearing distance of the cabin which I had wrecked, and in five minutes, wrapped snugly in my blankets, I was sound asleep.

I have skipped over this brutal scene as quickly as I could. In all my life it is the thing of which I am least proud, but I must confess that even the next morning when I wakened I was not greatly repentant at once. Fighting, to a young man, is its own justification, in many ways. I had given them, as I saw it, fair play. They had the odds of three against one. For a time, I felt that it was a very considerable exploit.

So did the whole valley, which came to know of it when the doctor was brought in haste, before morning, to pay attention to Joe's badly injured throat that I had gripped. The news slipped out while he was there, and he went away filled with the story, and made the very most of it.

After that, there was a shadow over me. I had acted like a wild beast, and people declared that I would continue to act like one and, on some unhappy day, commit a wholesale murder that would go down in black for many a year. There had been a good deal of sympathy for me up to this time, but after that, for a long period, people had little use for me.

I fled from the posses which I knew would come to the mountains, and in those five days, living like an animal rather than a man, I had enough time to think over my affairs and think over Mike O'Rourke particularly. What I decided was that as soon as possible I must get down to her again and speak to her as humbly as she wished. Because I realized now that I could not live happily without her.

It was eleven days after my last interview with her, that I stood again under the trees before the O'Rourke house and gave the whistled signal—gave it again and again, and heard not a sound in response. Then a door opened, but it was the form of a man which was silhouetted against the light within, and not the slender figure of Mike herself.

A man's voice called: "Porfilo! Oh, Porfilo!"

It was O'Rourke himself. I had never seen his face in all the two years that I had known Mike. But I had heard his voice in the distance, and I knew it well enough now. I did not hesitate. I hurried across the open space and stood before that square-shouldered little man.

He looked up to me with his hands on his hips.

"Son," said he, "will you come inside and have a talk?"

"You've got bad news," said I. "I can listen to it just as well here in the dark."

"You've got sense," said he. "I've been listenin' every night for that whistle of yours. I figgered you'd be back again, no matter what Mike said."

"What did she say?" said I.

"It would worry you a bit, Porfilo, if I was to tell you. Because I figger that you're kind of fond of her."

"I love Mike!" said I.

"The devil!" said O'Rourke. "I knew it! But there ain't no way of figgerin' a girl. I never gave her mother no twelve-hundred-dollar hoss. But Mike, she's got a sort of a change of heart—for a while, at least."

"What did she say?" I asked him.

"That she don't expect to never see you no more, Porfilo."

I accepted this blow in silence simply because I was unable to speak.

"She told me," went on O'Rourke, "that if the worst come to the worst, and you come back here again and give her a signal—which she told me what it was—I was to come out and tell you that she didn't aim to see you again. That's why I answered you tonight!"

"She's inside and knows you're out here?" I asked him bitterly.

"No. She's gone up the valley to the schoolhouse. There's a dance there. Porfilo, I got to say that I'm sorry about this mess."

"It makes no difference," said I gloomily. "She could never have married an outlawed man!"

"Oh," said O'Rourke, "you'll come out on top in the end. The law ain't framed to get a gent with an honest heart. It won't get you, Porfilo!"

I left good-natured Pat O'Rourke with this kind assurance from him and headed up the valley at the best speed of my mule—that swinging, rhythmic gait, half amble and half trot, done with a sway of the body that gave the shambling creature almost the stride of a hard-galloping horse.

I knew the schoolhouse. It lay between two little villages eight miles away, with a steeple like a church's pricking against the side of the mountain behind it. All was in the full blast of a dance when I arrived. The orchestra was rasping out a two-step, and I heard the whispering sound of many feet sliding on the waxed floor.

I left Roanoke in a position with regard to the best means of escape if it came to a pinch—and that was through one of the big, open windows rather than the door, for it was my fixed determination to enter that room, see Mike with my own eyes, if she were there, and then get out of the place as best I could. If there were trouble, they were more apt to try to cut me off at the doors than at the windows.

So I chose a window on the side of the building. Beneath the trees, a short distance away, I left Roanoke. Then I used a handkerchief to whip the dust away from my clothes and my boots and started toward the door.

The jingling of my spurs attracted attention first. Men do not attend dances in spurs; not even in the West. As I passed through a shaft of light from the very window which I had chosen as my probable one for exit, the giggling of a girl in the shadows ceased, and I heard her subdued voice: "Why, that almost looks like Porfilo!"

"You're seein' things," said her witty escort.

I rounded the front of the building and pressed in among the men at the door.

I had not taken a step among that crowd at the door, before they gave way on either side of me with a little whisper of awe and fear, and somewhere at the side I heard a frightened murmur: "Porfilo!"

The two-step had ended, the people had scattered to the edges of the room, and now the orchestra was tuning up for the next waltz, and there was a grand bustle as the men left their last partners and searched for their next ones. But my glance went, like the needle to the north, straight to the shining red head of Mike O'Rourke and, beside her, the lofty form of Andrew Chase.

I saw that and I saw, moreover, that there were no other men clustering about her—Mike, who drew men as honey draws bees! I knew what that meant. She was too happy with her present partner to invite attention from other men.

A mist of black hate flushed across my eyes. I looked away and found the blue eyes of a golden-haired girl close by fixed wide upon me. The orchestra had begun the strains of the dance. Yonder girls and men were stepping onto the floor and beginning to spin away, but all this end of the big room was filled with standing, gaping couples, staring at me as though I had been a ghost.

In fact, with my rough clothes, none too clean, the great spurs on my heels, the cartridge belt strapped about me, and a heavy holstered gun hanging at either hip, the sombrero clapped upon my head to make me still taller, and my long, black hair projecting from beneath it—for it had not been cut for a month—I must have looked the part of a pirate.

Besides, to make me all the more vivid in their eyes, there was the tale of how I had smashed my way into the cabin of the Ricks brothers and beaten three men to insensibility; that story was hardly more than a week old. They stared at me as though the crimson stains were still visible.

I stepped past the gaping youngster who stood with the blue-eyed girl.

I simply said: "I don't have many chances to dance. Will you give up this turn with your partner, friend?"

He shrank from me with a sick grin, as though I had stuck a loaded gun under his nose. I shied my hat across the room and shook back my hair. I said to the girl:

"I'll promise to keep my spurs out of the way if you'll let me have this dance."

She had been a little pale when I stepped up to her, but Western girls are bred and raised to the understanding that, no matter how terrible men may be in their own element, with women they must be lambs or else pay the consequence; and now she suddenly laughed up at me.

"There's nothing in the world I'd rather do!" said she.

We stepped off into the dance. Something like a groan of wonder started behind us and circled the room. A hundred heads began to turn toward us.

"You're out of step! You're out of step!" cried my partner under her breath. "Seeing Margaret O'Rourke threw you out, I suppose!"

I took a firmer grip on myself and stepped into time with the music.

"You're a fine fellow," said I. "I don't care a rap what Margaret O'Rourke is doing."

"Ah, but I know!" said she.

"What's your name?"

"Jessie Calloway."

"Jessie, this is my first dance in two years, and probably my last dance in twenty more. I don't want to think about anything but the music and you."

After that, she made it easy enough to forget the rest of the world. I shut out all thought of Mike O'Rourke, even if my heart of hearts were aching for her. I concentrated on that laughing, good-natured, freckle-nosed girl, and she repaid me. If I were not happy, she made me seem so. That was what I wanted—to make Mike understand that I could live very pleasantly without her.

It was a boy's thought, but I was only twenty. In another moment I was really having the time of my life.

There were not half a dozen other couples on the floor; and most of these were dancing automatically, while the rest of the crowd was banked along the edges of the hall and thick around the door, staring at this strange picture of the outlaw as he spun with the dance and his long, black hair floated out behind him.

It was more than mere watching, too. I saw some of the older and graver men drawing together in the doorway and then pushing their way through the crowd in front of them, and they carried drawn guns in their hands.

But that was not all. Most of all, I was conscious of Mike O'Rourke, dancing in the arms of Andrew Chase. Neither of them paid the slightest attention to me. It was all the more delightful because I knew that they were thinking of nothing but me. Mike was acting admirably, chatting and laughing as well as she could, but the face of Chase was a face of stone. Only his eyes held any emotion. He was fighting mad, I knew. For he had let the whole range of the mountains understand that he intended to blow my head off my body. Here I was dancing in the same room with him!

Of course, there was very little that he could do.

He could hardly stride up to me with level gun in the midst of the dance. Besides, the whole crowd was falling into the spirit of the thing. The old violinist, who had played for dances during half a lifetime, had climbed down from the teacher's platform—which was the musicians' pedestal—and now he advanced a little on the floor and began to play very pointedly for me, nodding and smiling to me with the end of his violin tucked under his old chin and turning toward me every time I swung into a different section of the hall.

"Look!" cried Jessie Calloway.

By the ill luck of the very devil, someone had managed to get word to Sheriff Lawton, who happened to be close by; and now here he was, coming with half a dozen men behind him. I swung Jessie toward the window and pretended not to see.

"Keep close to me—and they won't shoot!" said the brave youngster, and, though she was trembling, she never lost the beat.

Out of a circling spin of the waltz I stepped back suddenly under the very window itself. I caught up Jessie Calloway in my arms and kissed her in the sight of all of them—and then I leaped through the open window into the dark of the night.

I landed safely and sprinted straight down the side of the building and gained the shadows of the trees as two men leaned from that same window and opened fire.

They lost sight of me, and in ten strides I had reached Roanoke. Then off and away down the road to freedom; I flashed into view of the light in the opened doors of the building, now raging with excitement, and a score of people, catching sight of me, waved and raised a great cheer. It was sweet in the ears of Leon Porfilo, I swear!

Chapter Twenty-four

In Crothers Canyon

There was no real enmity between Sheriff Lawton and me. In fact, if it had not been that the law forced him to be against me, I know that we would have been the best of friends. But on this night, with all that crowd looking on, he would have done his best to get me, even if I had been his blood brother. If it had been merely brains against brains, no doubt he would have succeeded; but it was horse against Roanoke.

In the open the horses would have won, but there was no open. I saw to that. I put Roanoke straight at the hills, and he went up the first one at a gallop that killed off the sheriff's horse when he attempted to follow. Roanoke himself was breathing hoarsely when he gained the crest, but the sheriff's mount was fairly staggering, and before I had put another steep hill between me and Lawton, the pursuit was distanced. I let Roanoke drop to his wolf trot, and we glided smoothly through the night and away from trouble.

Altogether, it had been a foolishly spectacular adventure, but I was rather glad of the whole affair. It had given me another glimpse of Mike; it had show me Andrew Chase, and, somehow, I felt that after this night Chase would not appear such a perfect hero in her eyes.

I headed back for the high places, making a three-day detour to accomplish what I could have managed by a single half day of air-line riding. I dropped in at the house of Lefty Curtis who had at one time or another helped me in the way of picking trails, but was nevertheless a friend of Tex Cummins also.

He gave me a gloomy look which boded trouble, and Mrs. Lefty had no other greeting than a nod for me.

"Look here, Lefty," said I, "you mustn't treat me as if I were a thug come to hold you up. What's the matter?"

He avoided the question for a time, but afterward he said: "Tex Cummins has been to see me. He swears that you picked up the trail of Sam Moyer from my house."

"I picked it up above your house," said I. "If I meet Tex, I'll tell him so!"

"If you meet Tex," said Lefty with a sour grin, "you won't meet him alone. He means business this time, and he's going to give you a mite of trouble, Porfilo—mule or no mule! They tell me that the thing hops up the face of a cliff like a dog-gone kangaroo!"

"Never mind the mule. You ought to be glad that I found Sam. Because, when I left him, he told me to be sure to remember him to you."

"As far as Tex goes," said Lefty, "I ain't no slave of his. Besides, he'll know that I played square with him, if he thinks things over. Have you seen Chet O'Rourke yet?"

I knew that Chet O'Rourke was one of Mike's brothers,

but I had no more seen him than I had seen her father, up to four nights before, and I told Lefty as much.

"He came up here two days ago," said Lefty, "and he's been buzzing around that he expects to meet you in the Crothers Canyon any time before noon any day. He's waitin' there for you. Maybe the fool wants to get famous! Maybe he wants the blood money that's hangin' on you, old son!"

I spent that night with Lefty, gathering in the news, and there was plenty of it. Poor Lawton was half mad, it seemed. The governor had heard this last story about my appearance at the dance right under his nose.

Of course, I hadn't the least idea that Lawton was within miles of the dance. Who would have expected him to be? Indeed, it was only chance that had brought him there. The governor of the State had sent a telegram to Lawton:

Get Porfilo. Use every possible endeavor. Will give you military assistance if you need it. You are allow-ing Porfilo to make law and the State government ridiculous.

Lawton, in an ecstasy of shame and rage, wired back his resignation from his office, because some enterpris-ing newspaper had managed to lay its hands upon that telegram, and the result was that every newspaper in the State caught up this juicy morsel and spilled it in liberal capitals across the front pages. The governor had replied that he knew of no better man than Lawton for the post, and would consider it a shirking of duty if the latter left his post.

"And," said Lefty, "all that Lawton and his gang are doin' now is sittin' and prayin' that God'll be good enough to give 'em a crack at you. Lawton has wore out three hosses in three days. But he's just ridin' around in circles and gettin' nowhere!"

There were still echoes of the Sam Moyer affair, too. People on the whole seemed rather glad that the bank robber had been stripped of his plunder, but the law could not see it in that way. The only legal cognizance that was taken of the affair was that I had broken into the house of a citizen whose door was locked and who had insisted that I remain outside. Once inside, I had attacked "with intent to kill."

That was the whole thing done up in a nutshell! How could I make any answer to it? Sam Moyer disappeared from the adventure. There only remained the wrong that I had done to the Ricks brothers, and nothing at all was said of their guilt in having offered refuge knowingly to a violator of the law like Moyer.

"No matter what I do," I sighed to Lefty, "I get more and more in wrong."

"Not a bit, kid," said Lefty. "We know, and the rest of the bunch know, that you're square. If the governor is a flathead, does that really make any difference? Look here, Porfilo; if the whole bunch in the towns and the range really wanted to get you, don't you think that they'd do it pretty slick and easy? Sure they would! But it's only the sheriffs and a few head hunters that go after you. The rest of the boys sit back and wish you luck. They know that you ain't out to bother no honest man that is mindin' his own business. You think they ain't took note that you make your money off the crooks and the thugs?"

I had never thought of that before. But, as a matter of fact, I had always been received in a very friendly manner. I had the instance of my adventure in the schoolhouse dance, when half a hundred armed men had let me remain in a room for three minutes without raising a hand to get me. If they really felt that I was an enemy to society, I could not have lasted three seconds. They were afraid of me, naturally, because there had been so much talk, and because they never knew what I was going to do next, but they did not actually hate me.

The next morning I started at once for the Crothers Canyon. I had no expectation of trouble from Chet. I knew that he was a high-spirited youngster—a great deal too high-spirited to please his family, in fact. But, nevertheless, there was little chance that he would be waiting in the canyon to fight me hand to hand—even though the mountaineers had an idea that that was his purpose.

I rode to the edge of the canyon, however, and looked over it. Half a mile to the right, I saw a man sitting in the shade of a tree with his horse beside him, and I guessed that to be O'Rourke. I looked up and down the valley, but there was no sign of an ambuscade.

Sheriff Lawton considered me a good deal of a fool in many ways, but even Lawton did not think that I would be so foolhardy as to accept such an open invitation as young O'Rourke had extended to me.

I sent Roanoke down the bluff like an avalanche, and trotted down to chat with Mike's brother, if it were he.

Even from a distance it was easy to see that this was the right man. For his hat was off and a patch of sun, dropping through the branches of the oak tree, shone upon a flaming red head—not the auburn hair of Mike, but purest flame. Certainly this was an O'Rourke.

He climbed into his saddle and came to meet me, and when he drew nearer I was a little shocked by the look of him. He was as ugly as Mike was pretty. A typical "mug" was the face of Chet O'Rourke. He came to me with a vast grin, and his hand stretched out.

"Some of these birds in the mountains around here," said he, "figger that I'm layin' out to get a crack at you, Porfilo. But I ain't a fool. I hope you figgered that none of that talk started with me?"

"I didn't think that," said I. "But I wondered what I could do for you?"

"For me, you could give me a chance to have a slant at you. It's worth while! Lemme see the backs of your hands!"

I wondered at him a little and held them out to him, one by one—big, shapeless paws they are to this day.

"Dog-gone my heart!" said Chet O'Rourke. "I wouldn't believe it if I hadn't seen it for myself! I seen the faces that you put on Joe and Willie Ricks. I figgered that you must have slammed 'em with a club, but they swore that it was only your fists.

"But here I can see for myself that your knuckles ain't even skinned. That's something worth seeing, Porfilo. What are your hands made of? Iron?"

I felt that he was chaffing me a little, but then I saw that his foolish grin was caused only by his very real pleasure at being with me.

"I came out," he continued, "because Mike wants to see you, and wants to see you bad. What shall I tell her? That you'll come back?"

It was the pleasantest news that I had heard in many a day since my last parting with Mike. It went like a song through me.

"I'll ride back with you right now!" said I.

Chet O'Rourke laughed and shook his head.

"This plug of mine ain't no bird," said he. "I seen you come wingin' down into the valley a couple of minutes ago, and I know the way you travel on that Roanoke mule. Lawton says that the Negro that give it to you ought to be hanged for bein' a public nuisance!"

"I'm starting now, then," said I.

"So long, old-timer. I hear that Cummins is swarmin' through these parts, tryin' to get even with you for what you done to his man, Moyer."

"Thanks," said I. "I'll try to dodge Tex."

He laughed joyously, as though I were having my little joke—as though it were most absurd to think of me trying to avoid any man or group of men in the world.

Although I was a happy fellow to be bound for another meeting with Mike, yet I was thoughtful and pretty blue, riding across the hills on that day. For I could not help telling myself that if other people felt about me as young O'Rourke did, I was not a great distance away from a calamity.

They had put me up on too high a pedestal, and I knew that a man cannot stay on the heights very long without having an excellent chance to tumble down and break his neck. Chance and a great deal of gossip had made me into a giant in the imaginings of most of the mountain folk, and the knowledge of how they felt made me realize more bitterly just what an ordinary fellow I was.

I suppose that some people would have been elated; and, from time to time, I had been pleased myself with the respect which strong men felt for me. But now it was becoming a great burden. Before long, every man would regard me as O'Rourke did. Every other word I spoke, if it were not perfectly courteous, would be considered as a bit of high-handedness; and I would be surrounded by men who felt it was their duty to fight me to save their self-respect!

It was rather an odd thing. At the very time when men were saying that I was invincible and heaping up instances to prove it, I felt that I had my back to the wall. At the very time when it was said that I feared no living man or group of men, I lived in constant terror of the next five minutes.

Because I was in that terror, I had to practice every day. This very afternoon, riding hard to come to the woman I loved, I had to pause and for an hour and a half work until both my guns were hot, and I had fired away many pounds of powder and lead. I had to work from horseback at the stand, at the trot, and at the gallop, snapping shots at a rock fifty yards away—then making a trip to inspect it.

I would say to myself, if I had struck it five times and missed once: "I have killed five men, and I have been killed once."

That was the attitude that was forced upon me, and every time I gripped the delicately set trigger with my forefinger I told myself that I was shooting to kill or to be killed! When one has that attitude, one's marksmanship improves by leaps and bounds; but how frightful is the nervous strain!

Chapter Twenty-five

To Kill

But, by the time I reached the valley, in the cool dusk of the day, my spirits rose. I think it is impossible to look on the stars and the deep night sky without a lifting heart. Moreover, I had Mike waiting for me at the end of the trail!

I kept Roanoke in the trees among the foothills, gnawing my lip with impatience while the day faded from the mountains. The upper peaks were still rosy, but the valley was thick with shadow when I decided to cross it. So I shot Roanoke away at his driving trot which swayed us over the miles like the sliding of water down a steep flume, effortless and soundless, for those hard, shuffling hoofs never flipped down against the ground like the hoofs of a trotting horse of hot blood.

We shot up the mouth of the ravine, and I reached the accustomed trysting place under the trees opposite the O'Rourke house. I whistled the signal—and in an instant

228

she was out of the house, and hurrying toward me. Half my happiness went out when I heard her calm voice:

"Will you come inside, Leon? Of course, the family knows all about how you've been coming to see me. I had to tell dad a little while ago, you know. Only I want to thank you, first, for coming to me at all!"

I could not answer. Such coldness was worse to me than no reception at all! However, I swallowed hard and set my teeth.

She took me into the parlor. It was a little, square room, all full of bright-colored window curtains, and a little rug with huge flowers on the floor, and a piano in the corner, dipping down with the dip of the crooked floor level, and photographs of the O'Rourke ancestors framed under glass on the wall—men with great, flaring mustaches and girls watching the camera with a scared look, and two or three vases with narrow throats, crowded with flowers. It was all so feminine and delicate and looked so beautiful to me, that I hardly knew where to stand or where to sit or how to hold my hands.

"He's here!" called Mike.

A little, gray-haired woman hobbled into the doorway and smiled in a frightened way at me, and behind her there was a tall, blond-headed boy—Mike's brother, as I could tell by his face. For he had her look; he was not a funny cartoon of a man like Chet.

"This is my mother, Leon," said Mike.

She gave her hand a rub on her apron—she was ruddy from the heat of the kitchen—and she came to me, nodding and smiling.

"Margaret has told me such a heap about you—Mr. Porfilo. I'm sure I'm mighty glad to see you."

I loved that little, bent woman. I held her hand for a moment and wished that I could lift every burden from her

tired shoulders. I don't know why it was, but I thought
suddenly of the worn face and the steady eyes of Father
McGuire. Perhaps it was because there was so much
goodness in both of them.

"And here's my brother, Tom!"

The handsome blond youngster came up and gave me
his hand, and all the while his excited eyes went over me,
and up and down, measuring me, weighing me, noting
my big hands and my bull neck and my blunt, fighting face.

Why should I call him a youngster, when he was a full
two or three years older than I? But he *was* a youngster,
after all, in comparison. He was a manly chap, to be sure,
but he had a smooth, well-kept look; he had that air about
him which only a woman's care gives to a young man. His
eyes were softer and wider than the eyes of a man who has
been through the sort of hell that I had seen for more than
two long years.

Ten minutes of the sort of target practice which I gave
myself every day—life-and-death stuff—had more actual
soul friction in it than he had known in his twenty-two
years of existence, I suppose. I looked at him as I would
have looked at a child, but in spite of his good looks, I
liked him less than I had liked his ugly brother, Chet. A
handsome face is something which I can't help suspecting
in a man. The sort of flattery which it is apt to bring him
is not good for the soul.

He had plenty of strength in his grip, and he used all of
it, as though he wanted to show me how much of a man
he was.

I said: "Hold on, Tom! You're breaking my hand!"

They all laughed at that, and Tom looked as flushed
and pleased as a girl with a new dress or a boy with a
new pair of shoes. That silly little compliment set him up

on end. Old O'Rourke merely glanced in from the other room and waved his stubby pipe at me.

"Hello, Porfilo," he called. "Don't let that girl of mine make you too dog-gone serious!"

"What a thing to say!" said Mike.

But, though she smiled, I could see that she didn't like that remark. She shooed the rest of her family out of the room, then, and closed the door behind them. Then she perched herself on the piano bench and frowned thoughtfully at me.

"Aren't you going to sit down, Leon?" said she.

I remembered myself suddenly and sat down so hard that the chair groaned under me. Then I grew red and hot; I was conscious, all at once, of the dust on me—the dust even in my long, black hair and the unwashed look I had. I was conscious of the heavy cartridge belt around my hips by the way the holsters jammed against the seat of the chair. Mike looked wonderfully clean and fresh and dainty—like a new-laundered frock with a bit of scent sprinkled on it.

Then I saw that she was smiling at me with her level eyes—that crooked smile that drilled a dimple deep in the center of one cheek.

"You're not comfortable, Leon," said she.

"Not a bit!" said I.

"Well," said she, "you're a baby."

"I suppose I am," said I gloomily.

"But a nice baby," said Mike.

I roused myself a little. "You got a mean way of talking down to me, Mike," said I. "Will you quit it?"

She stopped smiling—in order to laugh.

"How did you like Chet?" said she.

"He's a fine chap," said I.

"You're saying that to flatter me."

It angered me a little, so much assurance in her. I could not help breaking out: "No, not a bit! What he's got is his own—and all his own!"

"Are you very cross, Leon?" said she.

"I am very cross, Margaret," said I, mimicking her as savagely as I could.

"Why?"

"I've ridden all day like the devil to get to you, and I've been feeling like a man just half a step away from a hangman's rope—but hoping for a reprieve, you see! Now I get to you, and you treat me like a side show for a while and then like a little boy for the rest of the time. I want you to pretend that I'm grown up, if you don't mind."

"I'll try to do whatever you want, Leon," said she. "In the first place, I want to ask you if you would do anything reasonable to avoid meeting Andrew Chase?"

"Honestly?"

"Tell me honestly."

"I'd do nearly anything in the world, Mike. I don't mind saying that I'm afraid of that man."

"I know that you're not *really* afraid," said Mike. "But I also know that, sooner or later, you two are sure to meet, and when you do there'll probably be a double killing. I can't imagine anything in the world beating either of you! Well, I've made Andrew promise that he'll leave your trail and go back to Mendez for six months, if you'll promise not to see me during that time. I sent for you today to ask you if you'd give me that promise."

It was rather a startler. I blinked at Mike like a child at a school-teacher.

"For whose sake are you doing it?" I blurted out very untactfully, and she grew crimson.

"Because I like you both, of course," said Mike.

"Look here," said I. "You want frank talk, don't you, and, talking frankly, I've got to ask you to see that I haven't much of a chance to live another six months. They're pretty hot after me."

"They haven't cornered you for two years, and you know it!" said Mike.

"That's all very true. But it simply means that I've used up most of my good luck. By the time the six months are over, the chances are about ten to one that I'll be under the sod or behind the bars waiting for a hanging day. That's talking from the shoulder. Then all that Andrew is doing is putting off his lucky day. Doesn't it look that way to you?"

"You speak," said Mike huskily, "as if you thought I were doing a favor to Andrew!"

The torture in me came leaping out into words.

"You are!" I groaned. "You can't look me in the eye and tell me that you don't love him!"

"It's not true!" breathed Mike. "I don't love him, Leon! I swear I don't!"

"What are you so white about, then?" I snarled down at her. "What scares you so much? It's his safety that you're worrying over. It's Andrew that you're thinking about!"

She was shaking like a dead leaf and clinging to my big hands.

"Leon, dear," she said, "once you said that you loved me!"

"I said it once, and I said the truth. I'll always love you!"

"Then you won't want to kill me with grief. You're too big and too strong for that, and big, strong men are generous!"

"Tell me what you want," I asked heavily, for I saw that the worst was coming.

"I want you to swear that you'll not hunt him down."

"Tell me the truth first."

"What truth?"

"That you love him!"

Her eyes closed, and on her white face came a smile that made it beautiful in spite of her fear and her grief.

"I do love him with all my heart!" said she.

I brushed her away from me. Oh, if I could leave this thing unwritten!

"Curse him!" said I. "He's broken my life once and hounded me away from my home. Now he's sneaked into your heart and taken you away from me like a dirty thief. Hunt him down? I'll have him in my hands and kill him before the world is two days older!"

I started for the door. She threw herself in front of me with a scream and tried to hold me back, and a wild babbling of words stumbled from her lips. I brushed her aside again and rushed into the darkness.

Something told me that Andrew Chase must know that I was to interview Mike on this night, and that he would come before long to hear the result of the talk. Perhaps that movement of the lamp behind the parlor window even now was a signal to him. I waited in the shadow of a hedge, for I was frozen with anger.

I was not wrong. I knew the step of Andrew Chase long before I had a sight of him. The moon rode high behind a thin masking of wind-driven clouds, and now and again she dipped down through a crevice between clouds and gave the earth a flash of silver light. By such a flash as this I saw Andrew as he stepped through the gate. He was not a yard away as I rose beside him with my gun leveled.

He did not so much as start; neither was he foolish enough to attempt to master that weapon or touch his own. For if he had made such a foolish move he would have died, surely. There was no more mercy in me than in a stone.

He said simply: "You want to take it out on me, I see."

"Turn around and walk across the street and through the trees," I commanded him.

"Is it to be a more private murder?" said Andrew.

But he turned and walked as I bade him across the soft, thick dust of the street and into the shade of the trees. Roanoke snorted in recognition of me and fell in behind my heels. I directed Andrew through the dark of the forest for a full half mile, climbing up most of the time until we came to a place which I had seen before.

It was as perfectly arranged as though it had been planned for a battle. For thirty yards square the ground was covered with short, even grass. The sheep from the village knew that place and kept it eaten down as trimly as though a lawn mower worked regularly across the surface.

The heavens were with me. The wind, increasing in the upper sky and swinging to a different direction, I suppose, though there was only a soft breeze among the trees, scoured away the clouds, and now the clearing was awash with a brilliant moonlight almost as keen as day. Men who have not lived in the high mountains have no thought how clear moonlight can be!

"Now," said I, as I halted Chase, "how shall we fight?"

"My dear fellow," said he, though I think he started a little in relief as he discovered that it was to be a fair fight, after all, "my dear fellow, it makes not the slightest difference to me. Choose your own favorites. Whatever you choose, you are a dead man, Porfilo, if you dare to stand up to me!"

I more than half believed him. It was only the thought of what I was losing in Mike that nerved me. I had been half mad on the night that sent me lurching into the cabin of Ricks. I was half mad now, I suppose, with a cold ecstasy of battle fury working in me.

"I think you are lying," said I. "You have never handled a knife in your life. Would you stand up to me with knives, Andrew?"

He hesitated the split part of a second. "With the greatest pleasure," said he.

I laughed—a sound that jarred even on my own ears. "A bigger lie than before?" said I. "I throw a straight knife, Andrew. Will you admit that you are not ready for that sort of work?"

"Well, curse you," said he, with a touch of heat, "I admit it, then. The knife is not a fit weapon for a gentleman."

"But scoundrelly blackmail and bribery is," said I. "To buy a gunman to hunt down another man——" I could not continue.

"You really seem to believe that fable," said Andrew, without apparent concern.

"I do believe it," said I, but seeing him standing so straight and tall, and hearing his calm voice, a great deal of my surety in that matter left me. "But what else shall it be? You wear a gun, and I wear a gun. Do you wish to have it a matter of revolver play, Andrew?"

"Certainly," said he. "That will be perfect!"

"We would have to stand within thirty yards," I warned him, "and at that distance I could not miss."

"I am glad to take my chances," said he, as quietly as ever.

"Have you done your hours of practice every day?" I asked him.

"Hours?" said he, with a little start. "However, I am perfectly prepared for you, my friend. You cannot talk me out of it!"

"Ah, well, Andrew," said I, "there was a day when you knocked me senseless."

"You would never dare to stand to me, hand to hand," said he with a thrill of hunger in his voice.

"Dare?" said I. "You shall see!"

I warned him to stand quiet, and with my gun in the small of his back I searched his clothes and found two revolvers stowed neatly away, besides a small derringer that hung around his throat. Certainly he had been prepared for me!

I took them from him and threw them into the brush. Then I stripped off my own guns and my cartridge belt; I jerked off my boots and tossed all in a heap. I found Andrew shedding his coat, and now we faced one another, and I saw that he was laughing by the pale moonshine. He had never seemed so handsome or so tall.

"Porfilo! Porfilo!" laughed he. "What a jackass you are to give yourself into my hands like this! Mike will be delighted when she finds that I am not only her lover, but a hero able to kill the great Porfilo with my bare hands!"

"Save your breath," said I, "because you'll need it. Only, Andrew, I wish that you would tell me the truth of one thing. It will do no harm to speak it, because only one of us will quit this place alive. Did you or did you not bribe Turk Niginski to murder me?"

"Why should I not tell you?" said he. "Of course I bribed him. If I had not, my foolish brother would have jumped into his grave trying to get even with you for the beatings you had given him."

"There was some other reason, Andrew," said I, with a bit of emotion in my throat. "I tell you no man in the world is such a complete devil that he would ruin the life of a boy of eighteen like that and drive him into danger of his life as you did!"

"How could I tell," said Andrew, frowning, "that Niginski would not only be beaten, but that his gun would disappear so that you could be charged with murder instead of self-defense?"

"But when that *did* happen, you let me go before the jury. You would have let them hang me, Chase, and never have lifted a hand to save me?"

"Why should I have accused myself and ruined my own life for the sake of a mongrel greaser?" said Andrew scornfully. "You have no sense of proportion, my lad. A gentleman has a certain debt of self-respect owing to himself!"

He had maddened me so that I leaped in at him with my hands open and my arms extended like any fool confident in his brute strength, but the fist of Andrew, like a straight-aimed rifle bullet, shot against my face.

It was a sledge-hammer stroke with all his weight behind it, and it rocked me back on my heels and sent me staggering. The whole side of my face turned numb and a wave of black mist rushed across my brain. Nausea seized the pit of my stomach. Never before had I felt such a blow!

Yet Andrew seemed more amazed than I. I suppose he had used that terrible right hand of his enough to feel that it was a sword of fire before which everything must go down; and now he saw me standing, though sadly staggered, to be sure.

He hesitated and lowered his arms for a single instant.

"My Lord," said he, "you're not down!"

Then he leaped at me like a tiger. I say that he leaped, because of the speed with which he came, but there was no blindness in his rush. He moved rather like a stalking cat than a springing one—as smooth as a dancer, incredibly light and quick, he darted in, always poised, his left arm well extended, jabbing me back and breaking down his guard, his grim right hand poised for the finishing stroke.

It would have been the end of me, I have no doubt, had he followed up his first advantage sooner, but his moment of pause had allowed my head to clear. I was in perfect trim. My life in the raw, clear mountain air, my days of hard riding and climbing, had turned me to flexible iron. When he loosed his right hand for the flooring punch, I had my wits about me enough to block it.

It was like raising one's arm against a flying battering-ram. The weight of that blow bruised the flesh of my forearm and raised a great swollen place on it, and the force of even that partially blocked stroke was sufficient to turn me half around. Then I fell in on him, ducked low, and got my two arms around his middle.

I locked them, and turned loose all the strength of nerve and body. I felt belly and ribs sink in under that pressure. The hands of Andrew Chase began to beat and tear blindly at my head.

"Ah—Lord!" I heard him gasp. "Fair fight—fists— Porfilo!"

I loosed him at once, and cast him away. I had had him on the verge of helplessness, and with the taste of that power in my heart—the wild, sweet taste of it—I thought that I should go mad with joy. The blood was running down my face from his first blow, and that side of my face was swelling rapidly and painfully, but I laughed like a drunkard.

"You're beaten, Andrew!" said I. "Get down on your knees and beg for mercy, and I'll let you live if you swear to leave the mountains and Mike forever!"

Chapter Twenty-six

The Fight Ends

He stood on the verge of the clearing, one hand resting against a sapling, his head fallen, dragging in breaths with a painful sound, and I let him get his wind again. It came back to him suddenly. His body swelled again to its full heroic size.

"Who would have thought it?" gasped out Chase. "Like an infernal bear! But you've had your last fling at me, my dear fellow. You'll never come within grip of me again!"

I had no intention of making it a wrestling match. For, since I had closed with him, the last fear of Andrew left me, and there remained only a vast confidence in my strength. If he wished straight fighting, stand up and fist to fist, he could have his desire. But now I went at him more coolly, with all the skill that Father McGuire had taught me in the old days in my mind.

He struck and danced away, and I waded in, taking

heavy punishment. I was not slow, but he was a will-o'-the-wisp. You have seen a dragon fly darting back and forth in the air of the garden, stopping in mid-drive and shooting back again without pause? Imagine two hundred and twenty pounds of dragon fly and you will have an idea of the uncanny grace and speed of Andrew Chase as he fought for his life.

Twenty times I smashed at him with all my power, and twenty times my huge fists plowed through the air while he side-stepped like a dancer and cuffed me with long-ranging punches. They cut my face as though he wore a knife edge across his knuckles, but he could not stun me or put me down; I was watching him too closely for that and playing for one opening—one opening.

I found it at last. He had flung up his guard a little in jumping back, and I brought a long right fairly under his heart. It dropped him upon his knees and jammed the breath out of his lungs with a great, loud gasp. There he hung, swaying, propped on one muscular arm, the other clasped about the hurt place.

"Have you had enough, Andrew?" I panted.

For answer he forced himself slowly to his feet and squared away, his face contorted with pain, but his guard still stiff and high. I rushed him, and the body blow had sapped the strength of his knees. I broke through that long guard and thudded a short blow against his chin. It snapped back his head as though his neck were broken and sent him reeling to the edge of the clearing.

Yet I backed away. I did not want to finish a half-stunned, weakened man.

"Take your time out," I advised him. "Take your time out and be easy with it! I don't want to beat a cripple!"

He had come up with a jar against a tree, and there he leaned with his head fallen back, his knees turned to water, his arms sagging at his side. I could have killed him with a blow, but, instead, I stood back and tasted the sweet relish of his helplessness with a brutal joy.

He must have remained there a full minute, and I could see the life begin to return to him; watch his knees hardening; see his chest swell with breath and power; note the lifting of his head. Then he leaped suddenly back at me and, before I was prepared, had clipped me across the jaw with a swinging blow. A little nearer the point of the chin and I should certainly have gone down immediately.

There was something treacherous about this tigerish attack, after the excellent fair play which I had given him, that maddened me. I damned him for a yellow dog and ran at him again. Twice I missed him with blows that would have stretched him senseless, I know. But as I drove at him a third time he stepped neatly and courageously inside my arm and whipped up his right hand of flame to my chin.

Like flame, indeed! A shower of sparks exploded before my eyes and I reeled backward, striking blindly to protect myself from him. His cry of joy was like the yelp of the wolf as it sees the bull totter. He came in lunging, desperately eager. Right and left he clipped me. I felt as though hammers were thudding against the base of my brain. My knees suddenly unsnapped and went loose. I was sinking toward the ground. My outstretched hands clutched at his body, but there was no strength in them. The numbed fingertips slid away, and I dropped upon my face.

I suppose that it was only an instant of unconsciousness. Then a ripping pain across my face forced me back to life. Andrew, who had pleaded for fair play; Andrew, who had begged for a stand-up fight, had gripped the back of my neck in both hands and was beating my face against a rock.

This was for life, indeed!

I twisted my body with all my force, and the suddenness of the move broke his grip. I reached for his arm and caught it with the power of a hard-screwed vise; with so much power that he cried out in fear and tore himself away. His own effort half lifted me to my feet, and I flung myself at his throat.

He retreated desperately before me, and there was terror in his face because of the silence of my fury and because by this time I suppose that my torn and bleeding face was a frightful thing to see in that white moonshine.

Twice, as he sprang back before my lunges and struck out, I saw him cast jerking glances over his shoulder, and I knew that he was prepared to take to his heels in another moment. I leaned in against a rain of blows that had all his power behind them, but there was no feeling in my body now. I walked through those flying fists as though they had been lightly stinging drops of water, and set my grip on his shoulder.

He could not break it. I felt the corded and writhing strength of that shoulder play beneath my hands as he strove to fling himself clear, and then I managed to clutch his other arm just above the wrist.

There was death in his face then, and just before I stepped in close and took him in both arms, he screamed with terror, as a man might scream when he feels the long tentacles of an octopus thrown about him.

So I laughed, close to the white face of Andrew, and then took him in my grip. I shook him as a cat shakes a rat, and all his body became loose.

It came dimly across my battered, reeling brain that he no longer fought back. I slumped to the ground and sat beside him, thinking it over with a sort of drunken solemnity, fumbling at obvious things. This was not the joy of which I had told myself. There should have been the strain of hand against hand and muscle against muscle to the last moment. But here was a man turned into a worthless mass of pulp!

And this was Andrew Chase, the handsome, the magnificent!

I laid a hand upon his heart, at first, and felt in an instant a feeble, fluttering pulse. He was still alive. It did not please me. I wished him dead with all my soul, and I knew now that I could not finish him while he was helpless. But something told me, as I looked into his white face, with the flesh loose and fallen upon it, that he would not be able to fight, not be able to stand, for some days to come.

I had not struck him often, but those few times had told a story. Where my fist had landed under his heart, withering his strength for the rest of the battle, no doubt the flesh was bruised and swollen. That was when the devil was raging hottest in me.

In the meantime, here was Andrew Chase, a very sick man. What should I do with him?

I thought of him then not as himself, but as Mike O'Rourke's man, and that thought started me into action. I picked up Andrew and slung him across the back of Roanoke. Then, steadying him with one hand, I guided the big mule down the hill, through the thick timber, and back to the village, and through the O'Rourke gate and up to their veranda itself. There I took him off and put him across my shoulder.

As I did that I squeezed a faint groan from his lungs. The door was before me. I struck it with my foot, tore the lock loose, and knocked it violently open. Inside, Mike and her mother, with blond-headed Tom O'Rourke behind them, came running. Three pairs of eyes widened at me.

I think that Mrs. O'Rourke fainted. At any rate, her face suddenly disappeared from before my dulled sight. I threw the loose body of Andrew on the bed.

"There's your man," said I to Mike, who could neither speak nor move. "Take care of him. He's not dead, but he ought to be!"

When she heard that he was living, it brought the life back to her. I saw her throw herself on her knees beside the couch. I heard her cry out to him and beg him to speak to her.

That, in some manner, affected my knees oddly and seemed to turn them as lifeless as cork. I went out of that house with dragging feet. At the door, a strong hand took me beneath the arm. I heard the crisp voice of Chet O'Rourke saying:

"Partner, you ain't fit to go on riding by yourself. You got to let me lend you a hand—come in here with me!"

I could not resist. He took me to the side door of the house and dumped me into a chair in the kitchen, and there I lay, a very sick man in body, and a sicker man in soul.

Chapter Twenty-seven

Giving Himself Up

Tom O'Rourke went from the front of the house to the back, not of a great deal of use to anyone. It was Mrs. O'Rourke who did the most. I think she divided her time between us. She herself washed my wounds and then swabbed them with iodine that jerked me straight up in my chair and made me sweat with agony. It was as though I had been bathed in living fire. After that, she bandaged the larger cuts and plastered the smaller ones. Then she stood back and looked at me.

"He'll do pretty well now," said Pat O'Rourke, puffing contentedly at his pipe. "That time the Geary boys got me down and beat me up, I was smashed worse'n this, I think. I went back to work the next day! But then they didn't hit with the weight of Andrew Chase behind their punches. He sure give you a dressin' down, my son!"

I asked him for whisky. He brought out a bottle, and I emptied a generous portion of it down my throat.

"This stuff is watered. It's no good!" said I.

"That's a lie and a loud lie," cried the Irishman. "I know, because I made it myself. It'll put some life and power under your belt!"

In fact, I found that I could stand up lightly enough, and that my wits were clearing fast. I asked for paper, pen, and ink, and when they were brought I wrote to Andrew Chase:

> You were down and out, Andrew, when I brought you in, as the O'Rourkes will tell you if you don't know anything about it yourself. We went out to kill each other if we could, and you did your best, as you know. I gave you your own choice of the way you cared to fight—and that when I had a pistol and the drop on you. We fought your own way, and as long as you wanted it fists, and nothing but fists, I fought that way, as you have to admit. You tried to trick me and to finish me by dirty work the first time you got me down. I wish to Heaven that I'd finished you when the luck turned my way. But that's ended and over. You're alive and you have Mike to make you well. But as soon as you can ride a horse, I expect you to get into a saddle and leave this part of the country—by yourself! I expect that you'll never come back.
>
> LEON PORFILO.

I sealed the envelope in which I put that letter and asked Chet O'Rourke to see that it got to the right place. Then I thanked the family for their care of me, and left the house with a silence behind me.

Why I was not taken within the next five minutes, I don't know, because I mounted Roanoke and trotted him slowly straight down the valley and then up the valley, and through two villages. The luck was with me simply because I did not care what happened to me, I suppose.

I was in the high country before the next dawn, and there I spent four long weeks, never going out farther than to find game. Roanoke grew fat and lazy. My wounds healed. Only a scar was left, red and angry, beside my right eye, and another over the left cheek, where I had felt the full force of one of Andrew's terrible blows, splitting the flesh away to the bone.

It was the lowest ebb of my entire life. Sharp summer storms were combing those heights, and with the howling of the wind around me I used to sit hour by hour and ponder my life as it had been and as it was apt to be.

I could see no joy before me. There seemed no purpose in an existence like mine, with my hand against all men and the hands of all other men against me.

So, at the end of those two dreary fortnights, I saddled tough Roanoke again and rode him north toward the house of Sheriff Lawton. It was such a storm as on that first night, two years and more before, when I had first reached his place and had entered it blindly to seek shelter. The cold of the wind made the newly closed scars on my face ache. Pain of the body was nothing to me then, however.

What made me cache Roanoke among the trees near the house I don't know, when I fully expected that I should never have a use for him again. But there, at any rate, I left him.

I went up to the front door of the sheriff's house. There was a sharp burst of laughter just as I came, and I felt, somehow, that society was having its mirth at my expense. Well, I was worth laughter, in my own eyes, as well as those of any other man.

I knocked heavily at the door and waited. It was opened by the sheriff himself. I heard him draw his breath through his teeth with a hissing sound, as he reached for his gun.

"There's no need of that, Lawton," said I. "I've come to give myself up. I'm tired of the game!"

He hung over me for a moment, studying me and saying never a word. Then he stepped outside into the night with me and closed the door behind him.

"You foller me," said Lawton, and led the way around the house to a side door, and through that door into his own room.

"Wait here," said he, and went out to speak to the others.

I could hear their voices raised in good-natured protest. These neighbors of his had ridden too far to relish a sudden end to the evening's entertainment. However, presently they were cleared out. Lawton appeared at the door of his room and beckoned me out into the living room, where I found the wreaths of tobacco smoke still hanging in the air.

The sheriff pointed to a chair by the stove. But I preferred to walk up and down the room, talking as I went.

"I'm through, Lawton," said I. "I'm finished. I've come in to——"

"Wait a minute," said the sheriff. "Take your time. There ain't anything gained by r'arin' around like this! Take your time. Lemme know what doctor sewed you all up? They said that Chase cut you up like he'd used a knife!"

In place of answering I asked, with a faint flare of interest: "Where is Chase?"

"In bed at the O'Rourke house," said the sheriff. He grinned in spite of himself.

"In bed!" cried I. "Still? What was wrong with him?"

"What was wrong with him?" murmured Lawton. "Aw, nothin' in particular. Any full-growed, man-sized man ought to of throwed off what was botherin' him. Except that the broken jawbone, it didn't knit any too quick. I guess because he was tryin' to talk too much."

"Broken jawbone?"

"I aim to guess that you're sort of surprised," said the sheriff with a deep sarcasm. "You figgered that you was just playin' around and sort of shadow boxin', I suppose—not really hittin' in earnest. But maybe Andrew's bones is sort of brittle. Because he's been troubled a mite with a pair of busted ribs, too."

"I don't believe it!" cried I.

"Most likely you don't," said he, "seein' as all you was doin' was sort of huggin' him a little by way of brotherly love. What? But that's what happened, just the same. Besides, his innards was shook pretty general, and the doctor figgers that another month in bed ain't gonna be any too much for him. That's the latest report that come up this way. His fever is gone, though."

It would have stretched any credulity to have felt that the results of the few solid blows I landed upon Andrew could have been so terrible. But I think that grief and rage worked together in me that night and turned me into more of a devil than a man.

The sheriff went on, as I mused:

"He was shook up so bad, as a matter of fact, that he talked a pile while he was delirious. Seems that he talked too much, in fact. When he gets onto his feet I dunno but that he may have to do a little talkin' in front of a judge and a jury!"

I gaped in earnest this time. "A jury? Andrew Chase? What the devil has he done?"

"Him?" murmured Lawton. "Why, hardly anything. He just played a quiet little sort of a joke one day. It didn't amount to nothin'. He just opened up and told about how he bought up the services of a gent named Niginski to go gunning for a thick-headed kid down in Mendez by the name of—lemme see—Porfilo was the name—maybe a greaser, by the sound of that name!"

His glance twinkled at me. I was too happy to take fire at the "greaser" implication.

"Lawton," I said, "then I'm clear! They've taken the whole thing off my head, and I'm a free man! Now I thank the Lord that——"

"Free?" said he.

"Why not?"

"There's the killing of Crane and Rudy Brown."

"Professional gun fighters, as every one in the mountains knows—with more murders on their records——"

"What does that matter? They weren't in jail—they weren't accused of nothing! They were hunting an outlaw by the name of Leon Porfilo, who resisted arrest and shot 'em down!"

I merely groaned. Then: "No jury would ever convict me for such things!" said I.

"D'you think so? Don't bank on it, though. Some juries are hard-boiled, I tell you! Particularly they're sort of set against burglary and the busting into of honest folks' houses."

"You mean the Ricks brothers? They were sheltering a bank robber, sheriff. You know that!"

"Were they? Did that give *you*—a dog-gone outlaw—the right to smash in on 'em? Did you have a warrant for an arrest, maybe? Did you have a warrant for assaultin' and batterin' three kindhearted gents sittin' peaceful around their fire?"

"Lawton, you're joking."

"I hope I am," said Lawton with a wonderful kindness. "I hope I am, son. There's nothing I'd rather have than to see you clear. But you've raised a pretty high smoke in your day. You've made a name that's been hot as hell in these parts. You've made enough trouble to get the governor worried and made him burn up the wires talkin' to his sheriffs and tellin' them what he thinks of the way they get crooks in the mountains. For two years you've lived and lived high off of stolen money!"

"Money that other crooks stole and, that I took out of their pockets. I've never taken a penny from an honest man. I can prove that, too!"

"No matter who took it first, you did the spending of money that didn't belong to you."

"Will they look at it like that?" said I faintly. "Well, I'll go down and face the music."

"I don't know how they'll look at it," said the sheriff as kindly as ever. "You'd be surprised at what a lot of fool talk there is goin' around about you since it was found out that that yaller cur, Chase, double-crossed you and put the blame of the murder of Niginski on your head. There's some that don't do nothin' but hike around the country makin' speeches to the boys about you.

"There's old Cam Tucker. He's makin' himself plum ridiculous the way he carries on. Accordin' to him, he never knowed but one real honest man in his life, and that man goes by the name of the outlaw, Leon Porfilo. There's others near as bad, includin' a sheriff that I could name," he concluded, "that's spent a lot of hossflesh and cussin', in his day, tryin' to nab you."

"God bless you, Lawton," said I.

"But now," said the sheriff, "what you're gonna do is to lie low and wait for advice. We're gonna see what the governor might do in the way of a pardon. Yes, sir, we're gonna try to clear you up pretty fine. In the meantime I refuse to make this here arrest, partly because you ain't of age, and partly because you ain't showed good sense in comin' down to tempt an old, broken-down man like Sheriff Lawton. Now get the devil out of here and wait till I send for you!"

I went, dizzy, but happy.

Max Brand is the best-known pen name of Frederick Faust, creator of Dr. Kildare, Destry, and many other fictional characters popular with readers and viewers worldwide. Faust wrote for a variety of audiences in many genres. His enormous output, totaling approximately 30 million words or the equivalent of 530 ordinary books, covered nearly every field: crime, fantasy, historical romance, espionage, Westerns, science fiction, adventure, animal stories, love, war, and fashionable society, big business and big medicine. Eighty motion pictures have been based on his work, along with many radio and television programs. For good measure, he also published four volumes of poetry. Perhaps no other author has reached more people in more different ways.

Born in Seattle in 1892, orphaned early, Faust grew up in the rural San Joaquin Valley of California. At Berkeley he became a student rebel and one-man literary movement, contributing prodigiously to all campus publications. Denied a degree because of unconventional conduct, he embarked on a series of adventures culminating in New York City, where after a period of near starvation he received simultaneous recognition as a serious poet and successful popular-prose writer. Later, he traveled widely, making his home in New York, then in Florence, and finally in Los Angeles.

Once the United States entered the Second World War, Faust abandoned his lucrative writing career and his work as a screenwriter to serve as a war correspondent with the infantry in Italy, despite his 51 years and a bad heart. He was killed during a night attack on a hilltop village held by the German army. New books based on magazine serials or unpublished manuscripts continue to appear. Alive and dead, he has averaged a new one every four months for 75 years. In the U.S. alone, nine publishers issue his work, plus many more in foreign countries. Yet, only recently have the full dimensions of this extraordinarily versatile and prolific writer come to be recognized and his stature as a protean literary figure in the Twentieth Century acknowledged. His popularity continues to grow throughout the world.

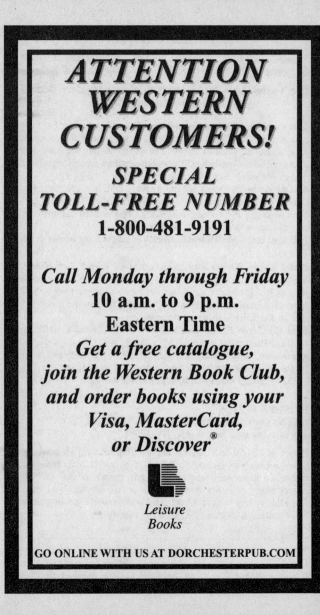